"Hello Gorgeous"

"Hello Gorgeous"

"Men, Sex, & Deception"
"The Dating Site Games We Play"

Sherry J. Cook

authorHOUSE®

AuthorHouse™
1663 Liberty Drive
Bloomington, IN 47403
www.authorhouse.com
Phone: 1-800-839-8640

Published by AuthorHouse   06/29/2012

ISBN: 978-1-4772-2775-6 (sc)
ISBN: 978-1-4772-2777-0 (hc)
ISBN: 978-1-4772-2776-3 (e)

Library of Congress Control Number: 2012911082

CONTENTS

INTRODUCTION

"Hello Gorgeous" was his pick-up line. Camille had fallen for it immediately.

How was she to know that Connery had been the same man she had viewed from her workplace windows months before?

Connery Jackson relocated to the Island after fleeing Louisiana and the destruction of the Katrina storm in 2005 and just prior to the deadly hurricane Ike, that hit Galveston in 2008.

Camille Bella had just moved into her vacation home after the Ike storm and the recent separation from her long time husband. She had just begun dating for the first time since high school and signed up with one of the free local dating sites for meeting men. Her taste in men was different now, from what they had been when she had married William thirty-nine years ago.

She decided to go all out, have the time of her life, holding back nothing and enjoy all the sex she could have. Connery would end up being much more than just a lover to Camille. Would he end up losing more than he anticipated? Only time would tell.

Camille was devastated with the news of her husband William, his affair and the embarrassment it caused her. She was having a difficult time living with the fact that William had been with someone else. Camille was on the road to destruction, and in the process could possibly destroy many lives, hers as well. But she never set out to destroy Connery's life, she adored him dearly, and was appreciative of all he had done for her since that day in June when they stowed away making love in her bedroom while on his lunch break on their very first encounter.

Who would have known that the entangled lives of Camille Bella and Connery Jackson would share so much in the future and it all started with those two little words "Hello Gorgeous".

"Hello Gorgeous"
In Loving Memory of
<u>Walter E. Welch</u>
Walter you would have so "gotten" this book. With
Your love of women and all your worldly adventures,
You of all men would have enjoyed this beyond my
Wildest imagination"

"Hello Gorgeous"
Is dedicated to my own, "Mr. Bond" My "Inspiration"
My "GCLST"
"Geographically Convenient Living Sex Toy"
With no regrets, you are forever a part of my life.

PREFACE

Camille had no idea where the journey might take her, but the thought of being with Connery no matter what the cost, was to temping to over look at the moment. Camille would find out soon enough that he might be completely out of her reach but she would give it all she could to win his love.

In the process of dating, Camille met many men in the first year alone. There would be weekends that she would date up to four different men at any given time. Things were getting complicated especially when several of the men had the same names, common names such as James, Jimmy or Jim. So she decided to keep a log of the men she was meeting. The log's list would consist of the men she met for drinks and dinner, and sex. Camille wanted to know just how many she could meet. How many she would have sex with. How many men would want her!

None of the encounters could take the place of losing William, the love of her life all those years, the only one she had ever loved. The things she'd done to try and save her marriage would damage her beyond recognition.

The men Camille met would offer her sex. For the moment sex was all she needed to reclaim her sanity. To know she was still desirable to a man, a real man.

This was the confirmation she sought. Knowing nothing else, if she could offer nothing more, she could at least offer sex to them all.

After time and many dates, Camille's log showed sixty-eight men she had met, had dinner with, but most of all, had sexual encounters with.

Connery would be the one she would grow to know the best the one she would end up being his, secret, "Jo Ellen." They would continue to have a lasting affair. Would it all be to no avail? The secrets they had shared together would become public in time and could destroy all they had built over the months. Camille's life could be forever changed.

Had Camille, known in the beginning, the events that would transpire she would have never set out to live this wild life style, or would she? Only to know she could possibly lose it all in the end.

More important would she lose Connery?

Camille Bella tells her story as it happened, event by event, date by date, man by man, the Sex, the Deception and the dating site games they all play.

CHAPTER 1

I always wanted to write a story, so when William and I divorced, and I began dating, I knew it was finally time to write. I was now free to tell of my many adventures, the good along with the bad. Knowing many lives would be changed after my book became public, for my eagerness to proclaim the affair I was having with Connery, in hopes of eventually winning his love, was all I longed for, and just maybe it was about to become a reality.

Because of my deep desire to write, to tell of my dating site adventures, many of my friends, co-workers, neighbors, family members and lovers would finally know my life as it played out over those years and how it evolved. Everyone would be able to read my words, know my thoughts, and feel my deepest desires. See the pain I had been through. The things I had endured as William's wife. The hurt and loneliness I had gone through and the happiness I had finally achieved and the love of the man I hoped I would eventually win as my own, and the other man, Connery, whom I would secretly always love, adore and forever desire to be with.

I decided to tell of my many encounters with the men I met on the dating sites exactly as they unfolded. The feelings I would develop for many of them and the one's that would become lasting friends. Confessing of my indiscretions with the men who only enjoyed me sexually and the ones that frequented my door even after years passed by, so many men I would never forget.

Connery was the one man, I wanted forever to be a part of his life, and he mine. Connery Jackson, was an attractive man, middle aged, and for obvious reasons available. I fell for his line from the beginning, but little did I know so would another woman, and our paths would cross in a most unusual situation. I eventually would find out about Connery's past, and his secret lifestyle, a lifestyle, well known to many women.

CHAPTER 2

"Hello gorgeous!" That was how he started every message that I received from him. He was clever with words, swift and charming. His online picture resembled that of James Bond. Bond's appearance and style had always been one of my most preferred looks in a man. When I saw him on the dating site weeks before, I had dreamt of meeting him, wondering what it might be like to know him, to be with him. My mind wandered, always wondering what kind of man he was. I knew I would never have a chance with him; I was not his type. He would require a more erudite woman than I was.

His eyes were blue and deep set. At a glimpse they appeared as if they could be looking into the soul of any woman that might be admiring his picture. He was fully clad in tux and tie as if he were attending an important function at the time the photo had been taken. His hair was salt and pepper and he sported a full beard, and mustache that was almost entirely gray. His facial hair was well groomed, trimmed to perfection. His skin was tan, as if he might be outside in the sun often. His smile was soft, and projected an enticing gentleness about him. His looks were what I had always liked in a man. I vowed that I would do all that I could to meet him, or just have a short conversation on the phone perhaps, just to hear his voice.

I knew a meeting most likely would never happen. So I would just continue to dream of him and always wonder what it might have been like to have been in his arms, to kiss his lips, to have him look into my eyes and to see my shameless desires to be one with him. I knew it would never happen. I just felt it in my soul.

After a few days of contemplation I decided to go a step further and send him a message on the dating site, asking to meet him. I compiled the message over and over again; it had to be just right. After assembling the words I wanted to use and after weeks of admiring his picture and countless instant messages, I finally decided to send him the request and a brief note. I wanted to him know how handsome I thought he was, as if he didn't know. What could it hurt, I had nothing to lose, and besides, I would just be giving him a compliment, a compliment among all the many I was sure he received daily. I desperately wanted to meet him.

I typed in the well selected words nervously, and then anxiously I hit the send button on the keyboard never expecting any type of reply.

To my astonishment, he replied,

"Hello gorgeous, how are you today?"

I couldn't believe my eyes! He must have been online at that very moment and saw my message immediately. I replied back to him, with some trepidation,

"Well hello handsome, how are you doing?"

He replied again. "Right now I am just enjoying how incredibly unique you are . . ." "YOU have no idea how wonderfully beautiful you are." "I so want to meet you . . . and meet you soon!"

CHAPTER 3

If Connery only knew how long I had waited to hear those words. I was so desperate to meet him. But my mind kept taking me back to the years with William and the hurt I had endured the last few months. So to have feelings so strongly for a man that I had never met yet was nothing shy of frightening to me at this moment. To want a man so desperately, a man that looked like Connery could be a dangerous move.

William and I had a wonderful marriage. He had been a wonderful husband, he had provided for me in every way. We shared the joy of children together and for obvious reasons I thought we were very much in love.

So I was crushed when William told me of his "other" life. I did all that I possibly could to hold the marriage together after his confession, but it was all in vain for it would end in destruction, hurt and unsurpassable pain. I tried every venue to keep the marriage in tact but when I walked in on William and his lover in those early morning hours I knew it was over I could never turn back, and must move forward from that day on.

Putting myself out there on the dating sites was something I had never dreamt I would ever be doing. But in this day and time that was about the only way to meet a man. Given the way society was now, if you didn't meet them in a bar or in church, the dating sites were the safest most effective way to go. But it was always a gamble and I would find out soon enough how the game was played. The sex games they all wanted to play. The deception so many of them hid until they had you in their arms.

Following the many disastrous, emotional months I had gone through, I finally decided to file for divorce. In August it would be final. After this difficult decision and much deliberation I decided I needed to get away, take a trip, and I knew the perfect place to go, a place where few would know me, or would be familiar with my situation. I could recompose my thoughts, my feelings, gain new direction. Knowing my life as I knew it now was virtually over and a new exciting one would soon begin.

Little did I know at this time, the events that would take place on my escape from reality! Or that, Connery Jackson, the man whom I had instant messaged for weeks and longed to meet so desperately, prior to my departure, I would finally get to meet upon my return!

I needed to tell my story, a story many other women I knew could relate to. For I knew many had gone through similar events as I had in my life, but I hadn't planned on destroying anyone's life.

The trip I planned drew closer and I left the security of my current life and drew strength from within and found a safe harbor to hide away in for as long as I saw fit. Leaving behind Connery and the messages we wrote daily, still having not met him. The fear of leaving for a long period of time made me wonder if he would still be on the dating site when I returned, only time would tell.

The events that took place for the next few weeks months and eventually year's, would be the direct result of my adventures on internet dating sites. And the remarkable acquaintances of all the many breathtaking, alluring sexy men I could ever meet.

CHAPTER 4

So with no specific date to meet with Connery as of yet and the divorce only weeks away, the option to just pack up and leave was the decision I finally went with. So this would be my vacation from reality, my escape to another world, a distraction from the deep desires to meet and be with Connery and a time to deliberate the loss of my husband. Free myself from the dating site for a short time and find myself. Contemplate the things I really wanted for my life and how to obtain them.

I had decided to make this an early summer vacation and visit the beaches of Central America. I planned out my trip, purchased my tickets, and readied myself for a month in the Caribbean sun. I packed the bare necessities and would purchase any other items I might need once I arrived at my destination. I was so ready to leave the city and get away for a while. I had decided to stay for at least a month and enjoy all that I could. I desperately needed some fun and romance in my life, something to shock my world, something out of the ordinary, some-one who could enjoy me as I was, without holding back, without any reservations.

I set out on this adventure not knowing what to expect in the weeks ahead, but I was ready and willing for whatever or whoever crossed my path. I had planned for visits in the rain-forest of Guatemala and the white sandy beaches of Belize and possibly a short stay in Roatan, Honduras, for snorkeling, if time allowed. I wanted very much to get away, and forget about what changes would be affecting my life in the near future. My life was about to change drastically, and I was afraid of being alone. I was dreading the fact that I would be losing so much, the man who had been beside me since my teen years, through all the heartaches, sorrows, and good times. I was afraid of not having a husband anymore. What would I do without a man by my side?

I had always had a husband, it seemed like; I had only been eighteen when I married and always had a man for all those things that a woman couldn't do. Life would be different from the way I knew it now, and I was well aware of what my losses would be.

The time spent on my vacation, my escape from reality had been a wonderful time, but little did I know when I left the States, that this time spent away would be the beginning of a new and fascinating era in my single life to come. Although thoughts of Connery never left my mind, I was always wondering if he would be there when I returned. The escape came and went before I realized it I was back home in the States, back to the real world.

Upon returning from this well-deserved, relaxing vacation that had lasted just over a month, I rested in my bed and reminisced over the events that happened in the past weeks. I had a wonderful time while on the beaches of Central America. I made many new friends while there, along with a torrid love affair, something I never factored into the equation. I had decided that it would be ridiculous not to live a little, since the men of my dreams, Connery and William, currently still my husband were doing no-telling-what while I was away.

The summer escape had brought me a surprise, Rolando Banchara, a beautiful man, the man I would indulge myself with for the time being. He was a perfect specimen, I thought, of what a Latin man should look like, to say the least. He had a rich, creamy, caramel-colored complexion, huge dark-brown eyes, fluttering long eyelashes, which any woman would die for, and perfectly spaced white teeth that appeared to almost sparkle when he smiled. His hair was dark brown with soft curls. It was not long, but not short. It was well groomed, but had a careless, tossed appearance to it as well. He also had a five o'clock shadow and a full mustache that encircled those perfect lips and white teeth. He had been on the shore when a local acquaintance and I had pulled up in the little boat, which we had borrowed from a neighbor, to take us to a parcel of property I had promised a friend in the States, I would visit while in Guatemala. I had noticed Rolando immediately.

I had come to look at the property that was for sale, and he was there to show me around. He spoke in a soft, kind voice, introducing himself to me as I climbed out of the boat onto the beach. He was quite intriguing and quite handsome. I instantly began imagining what it might be like to know a man of Latin culture intimately. Would it be different from any other man? Would his kisses be sweeter, softer? Would he know what a woman of society and sophistication would require? Could he deliver the goods? I had never been with a Latin man before and the thought was appealing.

I was pretty damn sure he would know how to handle any situation when it came to a woman! You could see his confidence in the way he moved his body, in his eyes, and when he spoke.

Rolando finished showing me around the property and told me about the many different plants and flowers, and even gathered cuttings from some of them for me to take back to my house where I was staying. The tour of the property had been informative and I would have plenty of information to forward to my friend in the

States and I was delighted to have met such a wonderful, attractive man in the process. Even though he was nowhere near as attractive as Connery, I compared the two in my mind inch by inch. Experiencing the lavishness being bestowed upon me by both and what it might feel like being meshed between the two of them at the same time. Heavenly is all that came to my mind.

The day had gotten extremely hot and I had not intended on being gone as long as I had. It was in the heat of the day now, and was past time for me to head back. We had completed the tour of the home and walked to the front of the house and back towards the pier. First Rolando offered me a cool glass of ice water and a chance to sit for a minute to cool down before I departed. The pounding sun would be very hot in the little wooden boat and fresh cool water would help with the short trip back in a refreshing way, he told me. We laughed and enjoyed the cool water together on the front lawn and spoke of the beautiful, glistening sea just beyond the property line and the towering concrete wall that protected the property from storms and rising water and how wonderful the sea could be on such a hot summer day.

Rolando finished all of his water, placed the glass down, and then turned and asked me if I would like to go for a swim with him before I left. I finished my water quickly, handed him my empty glass and as he placed it down beside his glass, I once again noticed his amazing good looks. He was tall and strong, with bulging muscles, and certainly at least ten years younger than I was. With no thought what-so-ever regarding my answer to his question, I slipped off my sundress, which revealed my golden tan body and the red bikini I was wearing underneath. I didn't have to say a word; from my actions, he knew I was all for the swim.

Together we silently walked towards the crystal clear water. Rolando assisted me down the steep sandy beach into the edge of the beautiful Caribbean Sea. He took me in his arms and together we walked out into the deeper, more, turquoise colored water. The feeling I was having at that very moment was if I were still a teenager having never touched a man, a real man, for the first time. I flushed with redness as if I were embarrassed to be seen with such a handsome younger man in public, dressed so scantly.

The rough crashing waves and the hot sun above made me feel unsteady and I struggled to stand alone in the salty sea water without his assistance. The beautiful white caps on the top of each approaching wave sparkled like due drops in the early morning hours that settles on the plants, and grass at dawn just the before the sun comes up.

We splashed in the cool refreshing water, and together slapped the waves at each other in delight, like silly child's play, while I held tight to his hands so not to fall down into the water. I laughed at him about his comments regarding how beautiful I was, if he only knew what I was thinking at the moment for I could not seem to take my eyes off of his magnificent body. Rolando's body was soft to the touch, tanned, and was very pleasing to the eye. His amazing beauty far exceeded my expectations of any man I had previously been with.

I didn't even seem to be concerned that this man could speak only a few words of English. With the look from our eyes, we could read and understand each other's thoughts easily. We swam for a while, when finally I became exhausted from fighting the strong waves, Rolando helped me back to the shore. We rested briefly, and then I told him I needed to leave for it would take me a while to get back to my house. He asked me in his broken English if he could come to visit me in the evening? I replied that I would enjoy a visit from him very much, and I would even prepare an America dinner for him if he would like that.

So an evening date was set. I was excited. I had never done anything like this before. Here I was in a faraway country alone, now having this sexy irresistible foreign man coming to my home for dinner. Was I insane, had I lost my mind? Why was I afraid? Rushing floods of concern for my safety raced through my mind for a brief moment, then I decided what would it matter, my life as I knew it was virtually over. So take a chance, whatever happened was meant to be, whether good or bad. This was my immediate conclusion and who knew, maybe he would be an awesome person. I had already been with many men back in the States and never had the fear of anything happening while alone with them. But this was different I was not back home and I had no way to call for help if this man tried to harm me in any way. What was meant to be would happen, and with no regrets I would suffer the consequences of the evening.

I arrived home at the cabin and began immediately to prepare the food items for the meal that we would be sharing. I decided to fry chicken, have sweet buttered carrots and make mashed potatoes. I would make tea for our drink, but had some Vodka and White Wine, along with some Patron, in the fridge if he would prefer liquor.

Rolando was to arrive at precisely seven p.m., and it was almost seven now. I bathed, and oiled my tanned body sufficiently. I brushed my hair, allowing it to hang long and soft on my shoulders. I put on some makeup to complete a more finished appearance and dabbed my body with the perfume that William, my husband, swore attracted any man towards me and made them mad with a wantonness to nibble away at my seemingly chocolate fragrant body.

I decided to wear a new aqua and blue bikini, which made my tanned skin appear to glow even more against the shades of turquoise and my sun drenched hair seem even blonder than what it was. I placed a clean pastel olive green sun dress over the suit so as not to be just in a swim suit for the dinner. The green of the dress made my green eyes greener than usual. I was anticipating we might go for a night swim so I wanted to be dressed and ready if he would consent to swimming.

Seven o'clock arrived and he was there, right on time. Hola, he spoke, as he entered into the house, through the wide, open, glass panel doors. The doors had been left open so that the evening breeze would flow through the house. I was so nervous now. Again, I wondered if I had just completely lost my mind. What would the night hold for us? Would I have a night to remember with this Latin dream boat?

I sat the place settings on the table and did my best to explain to him what foods I had prepared, asking him to please go ahead and fill his plate. I followed, filling my plate with a little of each dish. We sat at the new handmade dining table and chairs, I had just purchased from one of the local furniture builders in town. Rolando began to discuss the process of making such a wonderful piece of furniture. As he talked, he told me that furniture building was his trade, and the set we were sitting at was a magnificent piece of workmanship. The table and chairs were handmade, from local hard wood trees and would never need replacing. They were heavy, strong and sturdy, light in color and the builder had carved palm trees and sea gulls on the surface of them as a surprise.

As we ate, we talked more, but I noticed he wasn't eating much, so I was afraid he might not be enjoying the food items. Were they not spicy enough, not traditional enough? I hadn't known how to prepare the food of the land, so I had done as I had promised, and prepared him some-what traditional American meal. We completed all that we were going to eat, arose from the table and walked towards the open glass doors that led out onto the porch area at the front of the house.

The breeze off the Caribbean Sea was nice. The sky was lit up with a trillion stars, like twinkle lights on a Christmas tree. The backdrop of the stars was a dark, mysterious sky, inviting anyone to sit and enjoy such a beautiful sight. I couldn't help but wonder now if I really wanted to go for a swim or not. The thought of any scandalous exploitation might follow me back to the States, and how would I explain what I had done with this man if anyone were to find out.

We chatted briefly with broken English and my pitiful Spanish, but understanding each other seem to be easy enough, for our eyes expressed the words much clearer than any spoken words ever could. As we sat underneath the beautiful sky and the half-moon far above us, which reflected the stars upon the dark water, the thought now of a night swim was as far away from my thoughts as my home back in the States. Before I realized it, he took my hand and led me towards the beach and the water's edge. I moved slowly, cautiously with some consternation of what might be going on in this man's mind, as we approached the water's edge. He pulled me further out into water ever so slowly. I quickly turned my back towards his face and removed my sundress tossing it to the shore, exposing now only the colorful new swim suit I wore and my vibrant tan body. Rolando placed his large arms around my waist before I turned back to face him. He began softly kissing the back of my neck and shoulders. I liked this very much; I knew I wanted more of Rolando. His hands moved slowly up my waist to my breasts, he softly caressed my body. Kissing me with more intensity now, I felt my body fill with an amazing comfort that seemed way too familiar. I became restless suddenly, with a desire to have sex with Rolando. I needed a man inside me, and my body ached with desire! I'd known all along that I would accept his sexual challenge if it came to that, with no regrets. This is what I had desired to happen while on this venture, but I never dreamed of it happening quite like it was. I moved my arms towards my back, between Rolando's body and mine and untied my swim suit top and it fell slowly towards the water. Rolando's soft strong hands covered my breasts and he took me in his arms, turned me towards him and began kissing my body, my mouth with such tenderness, I couldn't remember when I had been kissed so softly. He was gently, slowly moving from my lips to my neck, suckling my breasts, and down my arms, kissing me with his luscious lips. He was in full control of his movements, with such power and an intensity that was difficult for me to resist. I kissed him back and together we removed the remainder of my swimsuit. I felt a sudden flutter in my stomach, a ping in my heart; this man wanted me, but why? I could close my eyes and dream of it being Connery if I wanted to, but the moment was too real to be a dream and besides I hoped that one day I might have the opportunity to actually lie with Connery, make beautiful love with him, having no other man in my thoughts but him when it happened.

Soon Rolando and I shifted from the deep water back to the more shallow water where the waves rushing ashore whispered softly with a gentle motion that added to the sensual intensity. Together we lay down in the water holding each other with bodies swelling with a desire to be one. The waves would take the swimsuits to the shore with the night current so there was no need to retrieve them at that moment. Time appeared to go by ever so slowly.

Rolando took my hand and raised me up from the water's edge, and together we walked back to the house. Once inside, without hesitation he reached for the fluffy, soft, down comforter, that had been in the chair. He placed it on the floor of the cabin just at the opening, where the breeze was felt at its best. As we lay down, holding each other tightly, kissing; suddenly he softly whispered to me, "Will you make love to me?" Without hesitation I consented to the act, wanting this beyond any means of the imagination. It had been weeks since I had been in such a heated moment of passion with a man. Even though there had many encounters since my separation none had given me the feeling like I was having right now.

Rolando got up from the comforter and moving towards his shorts he had pulled off prior to our swim. He removed from the pocket a condom. I thought to myself, what woman in her right mind, would decline such an opportunity as this, with this absolutely gorgeous man! I surely wasn't about to!

We fucked in the moon lit night, there on the hard wood floor of the beach cabin. Once the act of passion was completed we held each other tight for a while, each wanting more.

Together we relocated from the floor to the queen bed in the downstairs master bedroom dozing briefly and then the sex began again, this time with twice as much force than the first. Love making resumed with deep kissing and caressing. He had gone down on me and had placed his face in my crotch licking my clit, kissing me softly between my thighs and causing my body to exaggerate with convulsion like movements. He placed his tongue inside my pussy causing me to have an orgasm with just the touch of his lips. We shifted in the bed as I ravished myself with his large long dick and gently moving my mouth up and down on him as he held my head firm in his hands so as to guide me with the motion that he was wanting. This time Rolando preferred to take a more southerly route to please him and me. He rolled me over and raised my bottom high enough to insert swollen dick into my ass. Only on occasion, had I encountered a man that would delight in having anal sex, so I was tight and firm in this area. Rolando was gentle with slow but deliberate moves as he began his penetration. He was large and long and much to my surprise he slid in easily. Once completely inside me his moves in and out caused a rapid eruption of his hot fluids into my body, he came much quicker this time. For the second time, in less than two hours, I had sex with this incredible handsome Latin man. Ironically, I thought briefly of William but quickly dismissed the encroaching melancholy feeling that often overcame me when I wondered, how after so many years why I had married William. Though I loved him dearly, there always seemed to be something missing in our relationship, something I had never been able to put my finger on precisely. William had never wanted me sexually the way Rolando had on this night. He never, even in the beginning would have sex more than once in an evening, and never ever had attempted anal sex; he had never even cared for oral sex much. Sex with William was always good but never enough for me, never fully satisfying my needs.

I was physically exhausted and whispered to Rolando, I needed sleep. So I turned over but never felt him move away from my side. He lay there, holding me closely, as if he were protecting me from the night. Soft flowing panels of mosquito netting covered us completely and added another layer of sexual indulgence to the evening. As the netting fluttered softly in the breeze, the lit candle that glowed on the bedside table filled the room with a hint of sweet hyacinth fragrance. The pale, green, satin comforter was cool to the touch and felt good against my slightly sunburned body as I fell into a deep trance like sleep. It seemed like only a minute in time had passed, when I was awakened by the soft hands of Rolando touching me gently arousing me with his soft fingers rubbing my body, feeling inside my still wet cavity from the two acts of sex. I was aroused and awoke from my deep sleep. Opened my eyes slightly, just enough to see him approach my mouth, kissing me tenderly and causing me again to become hot with passion and wantonness for him. He mounted me again, but he pulled out softly, rapidly, and prematurely, suddenly he erupted all over my body. I loved when a man ejaculated on me; it was something I had always enjoyed, having these sweet fluids all about my body and then taking my partner and sharing the warm wet cum with his body. Rubbing together like flint and rock, igniting a fire. The fragrance of sex was strong and combined with the scent of the candle it made me think what it might be like to have made love in a flower garden where nothing but sweet scents abounded.

Sex took on many different scents but Rolando's was sweet, with a hint of coconut. Deliciously editable! I had never, ever in my life had such a night as this. I had been with several men since my separation with William, but none had been as good as this night with Rolando.

Even when William had invited others to join him and me, he had never shown such wanting desires to take me so many times in one evening. Nor had he ever taken me in so many different sexual positions as this night had given me. But he never minded others doing so, while he watched.

I had never dreamt of such a night of sex like I just had with this stranger, but I was pleased beyond words. This night had taken me to peaks of magnificent grandeur. I had been to the mountain top, and nothing less would ever be sufficient for me again. Rolando had set the standard I would require from all men, when it came to sex.

Wondering if Connery would be able to meet this standard or not, I imagined just by his looks alone he would be able come quite close if not exceed to a higher standard, if there could be one!

The third time, sex was quick, forceful, intense almost as if he was trying to prove to me he could do this again and again as many times as I would allow him to or as many times as I could take it. I wondered how many times I could last. Could I last another time, so many times so close together? I would hold on with a desire to be one with him for as long as I could physically manage. He was marvelous, in bed, and I was fulfilled beyond words. I couldn't believe where the night had gone, sex three times, each so different, so intense, so pleasurable for the both of us. Rest and sleep that's all I wanted now. Again I fell into a deep sleep. Not sure knowing exactly how long I had slept; Rolando again began to softly kiss my mouth, my neck, and the small of my back. This time upon awakening I stopped him, I told him, no, that I needed to shower to cool my body down. The night was hot, in many ways but my body temperature was insanely hot and I needed to be refreshed if we were to going to have mad animal like sex again before the sun came up!

So I got up from the bed and went into the bathroom and climbed into the oversized shower and much to my dismay Rolando walked in and joined me. What kind of a machine was the adorable Latin man? What was he made of? Why didn't men like him exist in the states, had I just not encountered one as of yet, given my apropos of bed partners to date? Most of the men I had been with sexually had showed constraint on occasion but when compared to Rolando each of them now seemed somewhat prudish. Rolando had been the most amazing thus far!

So we showered bathing each other and laughing together. He washed my blonde hair and told me many times he loved the touch of my hair and the smell of my shampoo. I allowed him to bathe me from top to bottom enjoying the experience completely, inside and out. Once done, and now loosely clothed, I poured us a glass of wine and we walked out of the house to the outdoors and were now enjoying the cool breeze on the front porch while lying in the hammock together. We spoke of how nice it had been to find each other and how neither of us had expected to have such an electrical experience together. We drank the entire bottle of wine and began the bottle of Vodka next; I was feeling drunk with alcohol and with a new lust for life.

After completing the wine and now almost half the bottle of vodka, this time I wanted sex I wanted to fuck Rolando again! I took his hand and led him back into the house to the bed and two of us went at it again. With all the strength I could muster I climbed on top of Rolando and rode him until he yelled out with relief as he once again climaxed, spewing deep inside me, screaming with sighs of agonizing pleasure.

It was now four in the morning and the fourth time our bodies had become one. Finally we were spent, and as well drunk with alcohol. We collapsed into a deep sleep, with the morning sun rise already on the horizon.

I had been fucked thousands of times but never experienced this act any other time in my life as I had this night. I couldn't even think of a word to describe what kind of night, and morning I had spent with Rolando. I thought to myself, would this be over with, would I ever see him again? I still had three weeks before leaving the Caribbean but I couldn't be concerned with this now, for my body ached and all I wanted was to be left alone to rest and recuperate from the monumental night of unbridled sex. So again I was swept away into a peaceful sleep dreaming of Connery, I couldn't get him out of my mind for some reason. I wanted to have a night like this with my Mr. Bond so bad, would it ever happen? Only time would tell.

CHAPTER 5

The vacation and weeks of carnal amusements were over. Finally I was home after an absolutely unbelievable time in Central America. During the flight and the long drive to my home I thought of the man whom I had fantasized about for weeks, wondering if he was still on the dating site. The closer I got to my home in Galveston the more I began to forget about the wonderful unconstrained nights and days of Rolando. My thoughts turned once again to the man I deeply desired, wondering if he would still be available, or was he already taken? I was feeling somewhat reluctant to get on line to view my email messages, afraid that the "Mr. Bond" who I so adored might be gone from the site. I pondered this question for a day or so after arriving home, before finally giving in and going on line.

When I finished reminiscing of the fabulous vacation I had enjoyed, and snapped back to reality, home, and the computer sitting there on my desk, and most of all, the dating site. I decided it was time, time to check my emails. Forget about the storybook adventure and accept my future as it was to be, alone, most likely for the rest of my life.

Messages, there must have been at least forty of them, just from men! Some of them were from men I had messaged before my trip, curious to know if I had returned yet. I figured I would have received messages from many of the men I had already been with prior to my absence, but most of these messages were from new men, men that viewed my profile and wanted to meet me. Some of them, their names, were ones that had stood out to me from the dating site, the handsome ones, some I had viewed but never messaged. There were messages from some men I would never be interested in; ones that just weren't my type, not the right look. There were messages from men just asking for sex, inquiring if I was that kind of a woman. Too many men to even go to the dating site and view their profiles just yet, but in time I would check each one of them out, and discard the ones unworthy of my attention and message the ones that appealed to me in some form or fashion.

I had a lot on my mind regarding the pending divorce, and my nerves were shaky, the unknown was eating me up inside. Reality had already set back in and I was feeling depression hovering over me once again. After another couple of days of recuperating from the long trip, I decided to read all the messages in my inbox on the dating website, hoping that it would take my mind off the divorce, and the wonderful memories of Rolando, and give me a boost of confidence, and mental energy to make it through the remainder of the summer.

Never expecting to see anyone online at that time of the day I felt sure I wouldn't have to chat with anyone. All I wanted to do was to see if "he" was still there and maybe check out some of the profiles of a few of the men I had gotten messages from.

There he was! Had he seen me? He had, and he sent his usual introduction message.

"Hello gorgeous!"

I was ecstatic and so surprised to see him online, I assumed he would have already found the love of his life, moved on and was off the dating site for good. But there he was! I had been on the dating site now for a little over a year and wanted to meet him so terribly bad since I had first viewed his online picture. I had viewed him for what seemed like weeks but never more than just a brief word or two had been exchanged between us via instant messages.

"My name is Connery . . . and it's marvelous to meet you, what is your name?"

"Camille!" I replied, sighing softly. He finally introduced himself to me.

I was in shock; his name was Connery, how unusual! Connery, what a strange thing, but so appropriate since he looked so much like Sean Connery, the name was fitting. It all happened so suddenly, I couldn't sit still. I wanted so to meet him, to visit with him, to know him; he was all I could think about.

CHAPTER 6

It was on the morning of, Friday June 26, Connery and I chatted on line briefly for a bit, I shared with him that I had been out of the country for the last month on an extended vacation and was so happy to see him still on the site. As we chatted on line for a few minutes I ask,

"When am I going to meet you?"

He replied, "What about today, around lunch time?"

I took a deep breath, was this really happening was I really going to get to meet this handsome man, the man I dreamt of being with for weeks on end?

I let him know that lunch time would be fine. Lunch time would be there quickly, and I needed to get dressed and prepare for his visit. He would be on his way to my home to meet me soon, too soon I was afraid. I was filled with such anticipation of his arrival I could barely contain myself. Thoughts of Rolando were history and all I could think of was how awesome it would be to finally be held in the arms of Connery, my own Mr. Bond!

Connery told me he worked very close to my home which would be convenient for the meeting at lunch time. I had shared my address with him and he knew exactly where the street was and would be able to find the house easily. Had he known where I lived at? Could he have seen me outside at some point? My street was a busy street and was a main drag for workers coming and going from work every day from the hospital compound as well as from the downtown area, and the ports. I wondered if he was employed at one of these businesses so close to my home. Maybe I would be finding out soon enough.

I agreed to meet him at my place, was this a smart idea? But I had requested that he wait for a bit so I could get dressed and looking beautiful for him. I wanted to look my best for the first time our eyes met.

His reply to me was, "God, you are soooo gorgeous . . ." "I want you for lunch . . . Hell, I want you NOW!!!"

My mind drifted away for a second. "He wanted me for lunch"? Hmm. Interesting concept for Rolando had wanted, and had me for dinner! Rolando's wish had come true and Connery's would most likely come true as well, only time would tell, for the lunch hour would be there before I realized it.

I couldn't believe my eyes, was I reading his words correct? I was about to meet him there in the privacy of my home. I thought would this be as I had hoped it would be a wonderful combining of two people into one? This time, with the man I had wanted secretly for weeks. But after such a hot steamy passionate month of Rolando I knew it would take a lot from this dream man, my "Mr. Bond" to begin to compare to what I had with the Latin lover. I had lost some of the deep desire to meet Connery while away on my summer trip, and my wonderful time spent with Rolando. But it wouldn't take long for my desires to be rekindled for the reality was that he would be here in a matter of minutes and I would know if he was the man that I had dreamed he would be.

For some unknown reason I felt the urge to ask Connery what he looked like. Was the picture that resembled Mr. Bond really him, was this what he really looked like? I had come across so many attractive men already on dating sites that had used fake pictures and as I thought about this, I now wondered, could this be the case with him? Why was he still available? He had such unbelievable good looks. What was his secret? I knew he must have several. Why would such a man of such revealing beauty be so available so approachable to a woman like me?

So I forwarded him the question regarding his looks and was waiting for his reply. I wanted to be certain that Connery was who he said he was and who he appeared to be in the picture he had posted on the dating site for all to see. I hit the send key, and then awaited his reply. The reply came.

"Give me your email address I can email you some pictures of me, of what I look like now." His message read.

So I forwarded the email address to him. Sitting there tense, uncertain what to expect from his soon to be reply with new and most likely current pictures of him. Anxiously I waited dying to see if he was as adorable as his picture on the dating website profile was. Then the email came, I hesitated to open it, as I did, there they were the updated pictures.

He was nothing at all like my dream man, nothing at all, not even a small resemblance to my ideal man, Mr. Bond. A stabbing pain went through me. I was disappointed to some degree. He had attached four pictures, one of which he had much longer hair and a full white beard. He had been wearing a pink shirt and the color reflected onto his cheeks which were full and rosy, the other picture showed him on the beaches with a sky blue shirt on which had accented his beautiful blue eyes. One picture was a much younger picture obliviously, for his hair was short and his beard was almost entirely dark, with very little gray at all, and as well there was a baby in the back ground, could this have been his baby, he had not mentioned a marriage or any children as of yet? Could this be part of the mystery this man was hiding, and why? The last picture looked like it had been recent but not sure how recent so I had to reply back to him,

"Which one of these do you resemble currently, if any?"

"The one in the blue shirt on the beach."

I felt somewhat relieved for he was still attractive enough for me to go through with the lunch date.

Connery wanted to know my response regarding his looks before he agreed to come over. He was certain that I would change my mind now that I had seen what he really looked like, he had deceived me, but was I still interested? I'm sure he hoped so!

I sent him an instant message sharing with him that he didn't look anything like the Bond picture but I still thought he was quite handsome and still wanted to meet him no matter.

"But you are so beautiful why would you be interested in me I look like Santa Claus and no one's interested in a man that looks like Santa?"

"Let me make that decision, ok?" I told him.

So I let him know that I still wanted to meet him, I wanted to see where this would lead if anywhere.

I had chatted with him online for weeks now and felt like the least I could do was meet him, if only this once, I felt I owed that to him as well as too myself. Maybe he would be a wonderful man, for I hadn't hesitated with the same decision to meet with Rolando at all. I had weeks of pleasure with Rolando while away, but now home, I knew I needed a man and soon.

Perhaps Connery had at one time looked like Bond if that on line picture was even really a picture of him. I would just make my mind up that he was an older Bond and his looks had changed. For his vocabulary and technique for flirting were still adorable and he had seemed so sincere and like a "real person" no matter what he looked like in the pictures he had portrayed to be or the ones he had emailed me as well.

Again he instant messaged me,

"Are you kidding me? I look old and fat . . . and you look like every man's dream!" Was his reply to my comment, in agreement to meet him, but he conceded and we were set for a lunch date at my house.

My thoughts took me some place I hadn't wanted to go. Why had he proclaimed to be someone he wasn't how many other things about him were going to be untrue as well? And why did he think I was so gorgeous?

I hurried to straighten up my home. Then hopped in the shower bathed and washed my bleached out shoulder length blonde hair. My body was tanned and still glowed from the month spent in the Caribbean sun and surf, and a radiance beamed from deep within as a woman fulfilled with all the sexual pleasure she could desire. I was much more self-assured now that men, some anyhow, would be interested in me, for that had already been proven to me by Rolando and seemingly by all the email requests I had gotten from the dating site during my absence. There were so many different men requesting to meet me I felt young and wanted if for nothing more than sex. Sex, the one thing I knew I could offer them all, and plenty of it.

I dressed quickly for the meeting; suddenly I noticed my hair was still damp. I had spent too much time on the house readying it for the visit instead of getting myself ready. Suddenly a knock, he was there, knocking on my front door! I actually panicked I was not sure if I was ready for him, I didn't even have on makeup yet. What was I going to do? I answered the door and invited him in and scowled at him for arriving so soon. I told him as he could see that I wasn't ready yet.

"I don't look like my picture!" Why did you get here so early it's not fair I wanted to be gorgeous for you! I don't like surprises so please don't ever do that again!

"Stop it you are gorgeous just the way you are."

And with that he handed me one long stem pink rose. I took the rose and thanked him and placed in the vase that sat on the table and thought to myself was the rose an apology for lying to me about what he really looked like, for using a profile picture of someone he wasn't?

I laughed nervously and told Connery that he would have to wait so I could at least dry my hair. So we sat down on the sofa and talked briefly and then I just jumped up told him I would be right back and headed to my bedroom. To my amazement he followed me, are you kidding, I thought to myself, really, what man would do such a thing on a first encounter, he had balls that was for sure.

Thank goodness I had made the bed and picked up the room some. Not that it would have mattered if I hadn't because he wasn't looking at my room he couldn't take his eyes off me.

Connery sat on the foot of my bed while I sat at the vanity and dried my hair, and then proceeded to apply some makeup. He kept asking me to stop but I continued to make myself up as best I could with him sitting there observing my every move. I even began to put rollers in my hair, what was I thinking, I was completely making a fool out of myself with Connery sitting there watching me, finally I stopped rolling my hair, and just turned and looked at him for all he could do was beg me to please not do anymore!

"You are gorgeous just like that!" He commented, once again.

I finally gave in to his request to just stop, as I stood, he took me in his arms and he kissed me for the very first time. I knew immediately this kiss, I would never forget for the rest of my life, no matter how many other men I kissed, Connery's kiss would forever be burned into my memory.

My eyes closed as his embrace surrounded me. I felt strangely safe, secure, and alive as our lips touched. Connery's kiss was soft, gentle, and sweet, his mouth was warm. It reminded me of a marshmallow, sweet and warm just as if it was beginning to melt over an open camp fire flame. No one except William, not even Rolando, had ever kissed me the way Connery was kissing me, something about such a soft wet kiss that made me always know that the man that could kiss like this was a man that I would want to be with.

But Williams kisses, even though had given me thirty-nine years of pleasure had only given me grief and heartache in the end. I wanted to think that I never expected this to happen like it was, but I was pleased that it was. As I kissed Connery back I felt him swell with pleasure, his penis was large and erect, firm, ready for what we both knew was about to happen, the soft groans coming from his mouth told me he wanted more. I felt the urge to give in to his desires as I wanted more myself. I had only been with one man the entire month while I had been in Central America so my body was aching and in need of a man. Connery would be the one I would melt into. I felt it in my bones.

CHAPTER 7

As we lied there together on my bed, not knowing exactly sure when we went from the standing position, to moving onto the bed all I could think about was this a dream or was I really lying here with this beautiful man. He was kissing my lips and my neck and slowly moving down my body gently, with utmost precision, unlike the tender forcefulness Rolando had used. Then he began to slowly unbutton my blouse revealing my soft, tanned, full breasts. I did not resist his actions, in fact I assisted him. I had not put on undergarments so once the blouse was unbuttoned my bare breasts were in full view for him to take as he so pleased. This was way too easy, too comfortable for me. What had become of me, when had I changed to such a nymphomaniac?

Things moved quickly. Before long we were in the mist of ball breaking sex. His body was warm and soft; he held me tenderly, so different from Rolando and all the other men I had been with, or was it just the way I felt, because he was all that I had been able to imagine he would be, all I had ever wanted in a man. There was something different about Connery's touch, experience most likely, but I couldn't quite put my finger on it, but I knew I would want him over and over again if for nothing else than just to kiss his sweet mouth. His kisses for certain took me to another place, a place I could stay forever.

Connery held me softly; I was filled with such delight. I had just had sex with the man I thought I would never even meet. I enjoyed running my fingers through his long gray curls and touching his handsome face and the beard that I loved, and ever so slightly touching his lips that was still wet from our passionate kisses. I felt fulfilled, I knew I could lie there all day with him holding him, talking softly, kissing and possibly making love again. I wasn't sure if he could perform like Rolando had so many times so close together but I was willing to give him the opportunity if he wanted to give it a shot!

How would he feel later? Would he think less of me for succumbing to his sexual desires on our first meeting, would he want more of me at some point? What kind of man was he really? I wondered, did he have a girlfriend, a lover, someone regular in his life, while we laid there after fucking, again my mind wandered back to the many times William and I had stayed in bed half the day making love, how lost I was going to be without him by my side. Tears welled up in my eyes just thinking about being alone the rest of my life and knowing somewhere deep down inside that Connery would never be mine alone, something just was missing, or was it just my imagination? Suddenly a thought came to my mind should have I demanded that he use a condom? It was too late the act was done. I had allowed this to happen so fast. I gasped, had all this been too fast?

"What's wrong?" He asked me, in a whisper as I rolled over and turned my back towards his face. As I considered answering him, I felt the warm fluids ooze from my vagina and onto the sheets, it was everywhere. It was if it had been week's maybe longer since he had allowed his body to erupt with such forcefulness. I was wet all over and wanted more. He had been so good, unbelievably good. I was so excited he had accepted my invitation to finally meet. My expectations were high but he had met my every need for the moment.

CHAPTER 8

He lay there languidly almost dozing when I ask, "Will you be back? Will I see you again?"

He answered me quickly, "Yes, but, I do have a request of you. I am going to demand that you take on other cock—even if I have to bring a second along to help me fuck you! Your pure sexual power overwhelms me, and I love it . . ."

"Seriously, for right now—I will be very satisfied with JUST our encounter's . . . But, believe me . . . That isn't going to last. It never does."

"Are you seeing others?" I asked.

Then laughingly I asked if he would see just me?

"Ha-ha . . . No guarantees." "You must see others as well,"

Why?

"All I am saying is I do not trust women who do not like sex with other men . . . Because then, it all gets back to the same thing—trying to make me into Mr. Right and happily ever after . . . and that I will never be for anyone, ever."

"As for others? Right now, I am saving all my cum for you . . . Ready to take it?"

The way he said that made me a little suspicious and I was a little taken back by this bold remark for it was difficult to ignore the connotation of the meaning and I wasn't sure at that point if I would see him again after a comment of that nature. He suddenly seemed so arrogant and self-assured it wasn't like he had been on the computer saying this to me, he was right there in my home, naked lying side by side. Had I make a mistake by inviting him over, having sex on the first encounter? How could I know? In time, I would know if I had made the right decision or not. His sexual allure was impressive and difficult to ignore.

Briefly I considered asking him to leave, not really knowing why exactly, but changed my mind rather quickly, after him taking me in his arms and again kissing me with so much passion. Instead I asked him if he could come back that evening after he had gotten off work. If there were no other reasons I had figured he might be willing to pay me another visit on the same day since he had proclaimed that I was so good in bed, and had fulfilled his every wish, and beyond.

I needed to be with him again and quickly. I needed confirmation and validation that I was wanted by a man, by this man. I knew I wanted more, much more, and I needed more. Once was just not enough I had to have him again and soon? Rolando had spoiled me the past month and sex was like food and I required it for my very existence. I knew I had been able to have a wide variety of men up to this date if I consented. For requests from the other men wanting to meet me were abundant. Many of these men loved showy large breasts which I had and was proud of and always revealed slightly in my online profile pictures for all of them to view.

But I had longed for this very moment in time and it had finally happened and I wanted nothing less than to be with Connery again, he was all I had imagined and more. Connery was who I wanted, and I wanted him bad!

The month of June was almost over and many things had transpired in my life the past months and now with the August divorce just around the corner I began to fear more of the future and being alone. Connery had entered my life at a perfect time and could be the man to keep me company in more ways than one.

July 4th weekend was the following weekend and Connery mentioned that he would be unavailable to see me during the holiday for he had to spend it with some of his family and friends at a beach party. He hadn't felt like he should invite me just yet to a gathering, were his exact words and was his excuse to go alone. I wondered what it was going to take to have him take me out on a real date, or to meet this mysterious family of his. I even wondered if there really even was a family. He was mysterious, too mysterious at times. Most of the men I had dated this past year were more than willing to take me out, to be seen with me in public, but not Connery. Why was I was already acting as if we had been seeing each other for months not like someone I had just met for the first time? Where were these feelings coming from, was it the thought of spending the holiday alone with no one to share it with, no grilled burgers no cold beer no fun times spent on the beach, would this be the future I would have spending all the special times alone?

So the 4th came and went. I went about my own business and the following workday after the holiday Connery called me again, he wanted to see me again, another opportunity to have a wonderful lunch break of sex. I thought maybe I should decline his offer but something inside of me just wouldn't allow me to say no just yet to him. I already adored him and so enjoyed his company even if it was just for an hour or so. Maybe in time he would be free to see me more, again this strange feeling came over me that this would most likely be all we would ever have together, sex at lunch. So we met for the second time and this time he fucked me like I had never been fucked before. Once again he presented me with a single long stem pink rose, was this his signature? He had never said a word; he had just handed it to me and then took me in his arms.

Once again I asked him to please come back after work; I was addicted to him like a drug addict that need more than one fix a day to survive. Or was I just addicted to sex, could it be?

CHAPTER 9

Connery had answered my question quickly with a response I hadn't even thought of. "Naw . . . my family is here and I have prep work for my class on Wednesday . . . and then, some work from home tonight as well."

Family, yes, he had "said" some of his family were here living with him. I had heard him correctly, so there was family here on the island, had he not wanted me to meet them and why? Was he ashamed of me, if so for what reason? All these thoughts went through my head one at a time wondering why? He mentioned one of the family members had been in the hospital near death and had just been released and he had to get home to see them before he went to his teaching position that night. He had told me that he taught class twice a week and on those nights he would never have enough time to stop by to see me after work. He said that there would never be enough time to be with me, like I would want and expect of him, on class nights. So I ask him more about his class but he wouldn't give me any more information regarding it. I wanted to know everything there was to know about him and would inquire at every opportunity to learn more.

"I prefer to stay your mystery man for now . . ." he told me.

"So positively you can't come by in the evening,"

"No, I can't make it tonight . . . too much going on . . . then class tomorrow again until nine thirty p.m . . . As well.

"What about next Thursday lunch?" He asked.

"Yes that would be wonderful I would love to see you again."

So Thursday it was, another date was planned to my surprise, the place and time would be at my home, and at the same time. I was fine with that just as long as I got to see my Mr. Bond again, and soon. I wasn't sure if I could wait till Thursday for after just our two encounters I wanted him every day, but I would have to settle for what time he would give me for now.

As we parted Connery said, "God, you are soooo gorgeous . . . !"

He kissed me passionately making me fill with excitement all over again. His kisses were wonderful and I could kiss him for hours on end if he would allow that.

The day passed slowly, and at times I would catch myself reminiscing, riveting from the fabulous time with Rolando while on vacation and now with my own Mr. Bond! I was amazed that I still had the knack for making myself desirable to men and that some men actually seemed to enjoy my sexuality and my openness. Afraid the days would pass slowly until Thursday and knowing that we would probably only communicate via instant messages, made me sad. I had seen him on Friday the week before and then on Monday but now waiting until Thursday seemed like an eternity. I had kept myself occupied on a date with a wonderful man, Franklin, over the weekend, after Franklin left, I just spent some peaceful alone time, a time I really needed.

Tuesday morning I climbed out of bed barely awake, but with an unparalleled excitement to get back online wanting to see if Connery would be there. I tried resisting, and decided to avoid getting online too early in the day so that I would not seem so anxious to chat with him.

About midmorning with an extreme amount of anxiousness I finally logged on and went to the dating site to see if he was there. He wasn't anywhere to be found. I sent a few emails and replies to other friends' and acquaintances and a few replies to new men requesting to meet me from the dating site. Then suddenly, there he was! He was sending me another instant message! How should I react, I thought? What would I talk to him about? I was so curious to know more about him so I began the new conversation by asking questions about him again. He had seemed so mysterious so recluse in some ways, this added another layer of intensity of wanting to learn more about him. Why was he on a dating site, why had he not been swept up by some wonderful sexy woman? Was there something more to this handsome man that he had not revealed in our brief encounters? As I received the instant message I read it slowly aloud,

"There you are gorgeous . . . !"

"God, you are soooo gorgeous . . ."

"Are you a good student? Or, do you misbehave?" *grin* "I want you for lunch . . . , Hell, I want you NOW!!!"

"I want to taste you again, over and over. You really are incredibly beautiful, so unexpected, and completely exciting!"

I was puzzled by his use of adjectives when describing me, and why he could even be interested in me, I had no idea. I toyed with the ludicrous and absurd thought that one day he might be mine. From the beginning he had always caused me to excite with an inexplicable smile even just with his words. I was just a normal middle class woman, soon to be divorced from a long marriage to my teenage sweetheart. The man I had loved all of my life, the only one, I had loved all those years. Things were different now for me, I was dating and had such a hunger for sex that all the men I met I had the desire to go there with them instantly.

Bond, he was different. I hadn't figured out how or why just yet, but I would.

"Why are you so mysterious why can't you share more of your life with me, more information about you?" I asked him.

He declined again any additional information, but he did reply,

"I am mysterious, I will never tell you everything about me but, "currently I have No mysterious projects as of late, so when do I get to work on you?" "Do I have to wait until Thursday, or could I come by tomorrow afternoon perhaps?"

I had to laugh out loud, but then replied "Well of course my mystery man you may see me Wednesday and as well Thursday again if you'd like, as we had planned?"

"How about some necking?" His message read.

Was he implying he wanted to see me again, today? Could that be possible, I thought. Avoiding the questions my mind drifted again to William, and thoughts of the marriage we still shared for just a few more weeks.

CHAPTER 10

Unexpectedly, Connery shows up out of the blue! No call, no email, no instant messages, no prior notice that he was coming by. What a surprise and a delightful one at that.

I met him at the door. He greeted me with a long wet passionate kiss as we embraced. I ushered him into the living room as I had for the previous two visits I sat down on the sofa and Connery sat in the oversized chair, hmm I wondered, why he had not sat beside me? Again he silently handed me another long stem pink rose. I accepted it with a simple thank you.

I couldn't help but think to myself, how could this be, the man of my dreams here again so soon, an unplanned visit, and already before even beginning a conversation he stated that he was coming back tomorrow, Wednesday . . . I hope he keeps coming, I thought to myself . . . he began talking telling me, wild and insane things that I would have never thought of.

"I would like take you to a secret Café down town, And to a hidden away favorite bar in the city and take you to a Park, to feed the ducks, and paint your toenails and take you shopping for a wonderful dress and take you somewhere special." "I want to take you to a wonderful hotel in town and lock us away in the room and make passionate love for the entire weekend."

I was floating on clouds imagining what that would be like, but again wondered why all of a sudden he had suggested such over the top ideas so abruptly. Then suddenly he began to give me some personal information regarding him; he had offered this without my questioning him about it this time. He had confessed that he had been married three times, had no children from any of the marriages, but he took complete care of his elderly parents. He had told me he enjoyed pets. What kind of pets, I wondered, real dogs and cats, or "women pets", was I just one of his so called pets now?

Now after all my previous questions he gives me all this information freely, where was this rendezvous headed? He continued to talk giving me more information. He now mentioned again bout his teaching but this time he told me taught multiple subjects at different times. That he was an adjunct professor and preferred teaching business over other subjects.

For some reason this made me feel better knowing a little bit more about him. Though he was still so mysterious in many ways, I was determined to find out what other deep dark secrets there were about him and why he had felt the need to keep whatever it was from me. Maybe we had not seen each other long enough for him to open up. Maybe he was not sure of me yet? Maybe he just didn't like sharing his life with his new acquaintances. I would never let up until I knew all there was to know!

"Come sit beside me" he insisted. So I moved from the sofa to the overstuffed chair beside him. He began to kiss me, this time with a little more force, more tenaciousness but still very passionately. He held me tight with his large strong hands, he rotated his body around me so that he was now standing over me, still kissing and touching me. He knelt down on his knees and asks me to remove my pants for him.

I did knowing what he was about to do. I slowly closed my eyes and my thoughts floated away. He caressed and kissed me oh so gently and his lips and tongue penetrated me. I was electrified with a gratifying predictable orgasmic feeling coming from deep within.

Then I noticed he began to undo his belt and unzip his dark trousers, I couldn't believe this, was he going to make love to me again for a third time? Had my dreams come true? Could Connery be even better than Rolando had been? Could he want sex everyday maybe more than once a day? At this point there seemed to be a slim possibility that he could.

Connery proceeded to drop his trousers and he looked me directly in the eyes. He had a hunger, a yearning look in his eyes, I knew what he wanted so I went down on him, and he placed his fully erect penis in my drooling wet mouth. I moved my lips and tongue around him and began to gently move up and down on him he grew more intense with his groans expelling from his mouth, groans of pleasure. Connery placed his hand on my head helping move his penis in and out of my mouth in a rhythm that was rapid and precise, and obviously very effective in order for him to get the most from the sexual experience, then with an unexpected force he shifted his body and caused my head to press against the wall. I didn't mind the pressure or if my neighbors might be able to hear my screams of ecstasy. My lips sucked him with soft slow movement as if I were licking an ice cream cone. Salvia oozed from around my mouth and then suddenly he erupted without warning. As he begun the rapid movement prior to the force from his eruption his body had shoved my head further into the window blinds, I couldn't move, I wondered, could someone possibly come to the front door, most likely not? But if so, there I would be my head in the window pane and a man's penis in my mouth with fresh ejaculation all over my face? It was an enormous amount and I let it slowly flow down my chin and he rapidly pulled himself out and he went to the bathroom and grabbed a hand towel and apologized he had expected me to swallow. As he began to wipe my face I looked up at him and smiled with pleasure. He kissed me again tasting the sex from both of us within our mouths.

Then just as he had unexpectedly showed up, he immediately said he had to get back to work so he pulled his pants up buckled his belt tucked his shirt in and kissed me once again, asking repeatedly if I was alright? Was I? I was fine I think, for the moment and nothing more than another unscheduled meeting would be all I could want for. I felt like I was falling for this man, but it was way too soon to have these feelings so what was it I was feeling?

Today had happened unplanned, unexpected and now he had expelled his hot sex within my mouth on our third meeting.

Again he told me, "I will be coming on Thursday as well." What would he want to do with me then I thought. I would not be certain but I hoped that it would be sex again. I had missed sex so much, since William had moved out; I was going to get all that I could while it was being offered to me whether expected or unexpected.

Sex, another day three times already, and he was coming back for the fourth time tomorrow. What kind of machine was this Connery Jackson? Could I live with this, could I allow myself to have sex every day? Was Connery the man I had longed for since the summer vacation with my Latin lover Rolando, the machine I had wondered if there were such a thing in the states? It was looking like he might be just that man!

Connery and I had chatted on line over the previous weekend following our first meeting, but I still felt his need to be so mysterious

45

and this was still bothering me. He hadn't called me at all from a cell phone or a land line he had not sent me an email nor had he given me any information as to where he lived other than that he lived very close to me.

This mysteriousness he projected, it was going to drive me insane. Why did he have to feel like he had to hide things from me? He had already told me what he had thought about me and how much he enjoyed having sex with me. I felt like I was the luckiest girl in the world right now and never wanted it to end. But his mystery whatever it was would get the best of me, I was afraid. Connery had to share more of his life with me soon.

That evening as I reviewed the incidents that had taken place over Friday, the weekend, Monday and now this unexpected visit on Tuesday and it was looking like another visit on Wednesday as well, I wondered where this was this going? Who else was he seeing, how much of his talk was real how much was fake, made up to make him look like he was a God was he really just a womanizer someone that had sex with any woman, my thoughts drifted as I fell fast asleep with the anxiousness that I had on the first meeting awaiting now for the fourth encounter with Mr. Bond my dream man.

Why does He think I am so awesome and the hottest woman he has ever been with, as I recalled some of his many comments?

I thought to myself, he's running a close race with Franklin whom I so terribly adored for all the right reasons.

I had been with Franklin on the weekend that Connery and I hadn't seen each other. Connery had used such lovely words to describe me, and I felt so indulged by all of the attention he had been giving me the past few days, but I had been seeing Franklin now for nine months and deep down my feelings were so strong for him. Franklin had been going through the toughest part of his divorce and was hurting badly. He hadn't wanted to commit to any type of relationship and now I wondered if this was why, because Connery would be the one I was meant to fall in love with?

As I awoke on Wednesday I immediately showered and made myself up to be as beautiful as I could. My tan was still glowing as was my face. The fact that I had sex three days out of the previous four astonished me and that there could be another day of passionate love making again, today, how could I not be glowing inside and out?

I hadn't realized how much I had missed all those years with my x the one I had given myself to for so long. Always afraid to yield to another if the opportunity arosc. I had loved him so much but the sex had waned in the last few years and I was having so much fun now. It was almost too good to be true. My girlfriends that I had shared the recent events with were so envious and couldn't believe that I was involved with not just one man, but now two and both so handsome and sexy. How had I managed to snag two men? When neither of them hadn't been able to get one, let alone two? They couldn't wait to hear about the latest rendezvous' with Connery. I wondered, did my friends think I was bragging I had only wanted them to know how happy I was. I felt I had deserved every minute of this, for no one had been through what I had just gone through, and no one could understand the feelings I had, the old ones and the new ones alike.

CHAPTER 11

The month of July was a month I would never forget, for Connery and I would meet almost every day, sometimes twice a day for sex. My wildest imagination would have never let me think the events I was going through would have happened. With so much on my mind the daily encounters with Connery kept me from dwelling on the inevitable pending divorce and the concerns that I would be facing afterwards. Money would be tight and I would need a full time job and what would I do with all the furnishings from the primary home I had shared with William for the past thirty-nine years? Which house would I choose to live in and make my permanent residence would I continue to live in the Galveston home as I had been since the storm, or would I just sell the one I ended up with and move on with my life and go elsewhere? All these things played heavy on my mind but now with Connery a big part of my life I didn't think I would be able to ever leave the island or him. Something would have to give eventually to make this relationship work or cause it to die. Which would it be?

Connery would take me to places I had never been, emotionally. He would take me in his arms, kiss me with unrestrained passion, do things to me physically no man had ever done.

The pleasure he gave me was indescribable. But there were other men as well, in fact many of them. Before I ever sent Connery one message, there had been at least thirty other men I had met, been with, or just talked to online.

Michael had been the first date, the very first one, after my decision to get on the dating site, seeking men with the hope to find my second, Mr. Right. He was a photographer of sorts and a salesman, which visited the island frequently.

Michael had contacted me on the dating site and we had set a date to meet at the Tiki Bar close to my home, I would meet him there vs. have him pick me up. I was petrified; it had been thirty-nine years since I had been on a date. How was I supposed to act, what if he wanted to kiss me, hold my hand. I know this was so stupid but it was how I was feeling and I was pretty sure Michael would notice my nervousness as well.

The time arrived for me to leave and meet him at the bar. I had decided to wear jeans and a nice shirt, carry a sweater since it would be cool out and the bar was an outside establishment, and if the wind was blowing it could get very cool in the evening hours. I arrived on time; there he was walking towards me. We hugged and introduced ourselves, then chose a table and talked as we sipped on margaritas. The evening was going very well, to my surprise. He was very nice, soft spoken, a tall, blonde headed man about my age and he sported the beard and mustache I so adored on my man. We sat and enjoyed a couple of drinks and then he asked me if I would like to go into town to a local club for a bit? Of course I told him I would like that very much so we decided to drop my car off at my house since it would be on the way and I would ride with him to the club. Up until this point he had only hugged me, held my hand, and thank goodness he had not tried to kiss me. I know my lips were shaking and my voice was probably trembling when I spoke but he didn't mention it at all.

We arrived at the club; he parked and walked me in, with his arms around me. I was feeling somewhat awkward but was determined to make this a nice evening and have a great time, no matter what it would take. We ordered Lemon Drop martini's and took a seat on the sofa to listen to the music the band was playing. It was still too early for there to be a large crowd at the club so it gave us ample opportunity to visit more, and see where the night would take us. I was beginning to feel a little tipsy since I had not eaten a bite in fear of feeling fat! The alcohol was rapidly breaking down my anxiety and I was finally loosening up the way I knew I should feel, for his sake if nothing else. We drank and talked and finally he leaned over towards me and as a gentleman would, and ask if he could kiss me, I replied yes you may, and that was the beginning of one crazy night.

We made out like to teenagers on the sofa as if no one else was in the room. I hadn't even noticed that the crowd was beginning to grow and the band was playing and people were dancing. I had relaxed so much that together Michael and I were almost in a prone position on the sofa. After an hour or so of light petting and kissing we decided we needed to leave the club and go somewhere more private. I was not taking him back to my place I knew that way before the date begin. I was no way ready to be with another man at this point and figured no man would even have the audacity to assume that I would want sex since I had just separated from William. When meeting these new men I had let them all know that this was very new to me, plainly speaking I would not tolerate a man that thought he would be having sex with me by any means on a first date. Little did I know I lied to myself and in the heat of passion, sex would consume my every thought, my entire being?

Michael and I left the club but he had no idea where we should go that would be private so we could pick up where we left off at in the club. So I decided we should take a walk on the beach and knew the perfect place to go. We would drive to the East End, where they had just completed a walkway from the new addition out onto the beach. No one was living in the homes as of yet nor would there be anyone on the beach, I hoped, at that particular location this time of night. We made our way to the beach and stepped out onto the sand, the water was sparkling like diamonds for the moon was full and it was as if we were in a spot light, a spot light put there just for us.

We laughed and played in the surf running from the waves as they rolled in to keep from getting our shoes wet. As we walked along he took me suddenly in his arms and began kissing me with such uninhibited passion. This was all so new for me, but he kissed very well, not as well as William, but good enough to arouse the inner sexual desires within me. He held me tight with his large hands and began to feel my breasts, rub them gently; I felt my body heat up with desire almost immediately. Kissing was not going to get the job done, but sex, actual intercourse just didn't seem right for some reason but the feeling I was having was almost too strong to withhold much longer. He raised my blouse and unhooked my bra as he kissed my nipples slightly tugging at them making them hard and erect with just one touch of his lips. He was swelling in his pants; I could feel his erection up against my legs. Oh my, what was I going to do? This feeling was so incredible I wanted him bad and he wanted me but as we discussed the fact of having sex, he commented that he had not come prepared and had never planned on this happening, not that he didn't want it to but that it hadn't crossed his mind to bring a condom. So as we stood there in the moonlight kissing, holding each other not saying a word. He unzipped his trousers and without a word, I kneeled down and began kissing him tugging on his penis with my mouth. He was seeping and whispered he was overcome with desire to have sex but without a condom he just wouldn't go that far. Which made me feel somewhat relieved that on a first date some men might just enjoy the date, and not just want to date for sex, but might actually have some respect for a woman still?

As we played with each other I had taken his dick in my hand, his trousers now falling down just about his knees, I was walking him like a dog on a leash down the beach. He laughed and told me he had never been led around anywhere by his dick before! But the act was making him feel erotic in a way like no other, asking if I had brought a collar he could wear, or a whip to spank him with as well. He was as submissive as he could be with my silly suggestions, telling him to bark for me and even asking him to get on his knees and crawl through the sand. All in good humor we laughed till we just couldn't laugh anymore and decided we needed to sit down desperately. We moved to the walkway and figured this would be as good as we could get since he didn't have a blanket or a towel in his car. I removed my sweater and laid it down on the wooden walk. As I turned back towards him, I was going to kiss him, but he was way ahead of me suddenly, he slowly slid his hands into my jeans, unsnapped the snap and unzipped the zipper and slowly tugged at them to slip down below my waist, and within an instant he was inside my body with his tongue, causing enormous orgasmic convulsions within my body. As he kissed and fingered me, I kept my hands on his dick so that I could continue to feel him harden with every passing second.

The mosquitos were franticly biting at our butts and legs, and we would most likely be covered in bites once we were done and left the beach. Time stood still as we tongued and licked and suckled each other's genitals, caressing each other in the moonlit night. Little to our dismay suddenly a beam of light approached the area close to where we were lying. Who was it? Would they see us, catch us in the act of oral sex in a public place? Fear overwhelmed me and as the light beam seemed to get closer we hurriedly pulled our pants up and put our shirts back on. I stuck my bra inside his jacket for there was not enough time to put it back on before the light would be directly on us. As we lay there still perfectly still, like headstones on a grave, the light seemed to be passing us over and moving on so we froze in our places until we knew for sure it was leaving. Soon enough it moved on further down the walk and we slowly stood up and decided it might be best to head towards the car before we were approached by the deputy, and arrested for indecent exposure. Even though no one else was anywhere near the site we could have been easily hauled off to jail in a heartbeat.

We climbed back into his car and sat there for a few minutes and laughed. What an experience this had been. Michael had ejaculated while on the walkway and his cum was all over my lower body, thighs and hands. He had tried to wipe as much off as he could with a napkin, he had for some reason placed in his pocket while at the bar. The relief I felt was amazing, I had gone on a date for the first time, given a strange man a blow job, allowed him to have oral sex with me and to ejaculate on me, all on the beach in the middle of the night. It was somewhat romantic, very erotic and all I could think of was why William hadn't ever made love with me this way. Why had William come to mind in such a strange time, I suppose I was wishing he would have been Michael and we were still together?

We left the beach and Michael drove me home. He walked me to the door kissed me goodnight and we said goodbye. I had no idea if I would ever see him again but knowing the next time he most likely would come prepared for full head on sex if we did.

I had deceived myself, I wanted to hold strong to my convictions regarding dating, sex, and anything to do with a situation, when put in a compromising sexual position, but I had failed, I had faltered, I had succumbed to a strange man's wants and desires, or was it me that had pushed this? Was it me, what was I doing, where was my life headed? This was just the beginning, the very first date! Little did I know that there would be many to follow and each would be so different, so exciting!

So my first experience with dating since high school was just as I figured it might be. Full of sexual activity and happening in places I would have never thought things of that nature would have taken place. What would the next date hold for me; would there be another date, a different man? How had I come to this place in my life, I had no idea. I wanted to blame it all on William; he had caused this all to happen. He had driven me to this point, to have sex with men, no matter who they were, or how long I had known them, nor where the act took place. I had disgusted myself I was ashamed and felt sick. What would I do, I had no one to turn to, no one to share these feelings with or question if this was what the dating scene was actually like now? Were all women expected to have oral sex, and intercourse, on the first date?

Michael had opened a door to a side of me I had never known. A part of me, that I figured was always inside, but had never had the opportunity to let it out, to be the sexual person I had been born to be.

But Connery, oh Connery, he was amazing, he had brought out the very best in me every time we were together. He was so gracious, kind, and so handsome, beyond words. Intelligent, sexy, and so unbelievable tender and gentle like no other I had been with. He was fun, so, so much fun! Such, "Gentle Fun."

CHAPTER **12**

Connery became a little evasive after so many weeks and the daily sexual encounters. We made time whenever we could to be together we both required more sex than once day, we were addicted, or at least I was. Something was wrong, different, still it was all good, but I could feel it, tell something was not right with him.

I was confused as to why he had gone back into his shell of sorts; the mysterious Connery was poking his head out again. I had decided to find out for myself what his deal was, see if there was a wife, a girlfriend, heck even a boyfriend, since that was always a consideration when it came to these dating site men. I would never automatically concede that every man was heterosexual again. Even though Connery and I had been seeing each other now for weeks, I still hadn't gotten a confirmation if he was with someone on permanent terms. I had been with him every day but was dating others too so the curiosity had not been so prevalent as it had been in the beginning, I simply hadn't cared so much anymore, for if there was another woman, well, I felt sorry for her. For surely I was getting all he had to give sexually, no man could have physically been able to keep this type of pace up with a girlfriend and still have supplied a wife, or whomever, with the sex that most would deem necessary for two people that were in a real relationship.

Or could they? I had to know! So I had put together a scheme with one of my closest guy friends to settle this once and for all.

On occasions I had shared my experiences with my close friend Caleb, regarding Connery. Caleb had mentioned to me that we should set up a sting operation of sorts and see if we could catch Connery and finally find out what this big secret was.

Caleb and I decided to dress in outlandish clothes and wear wigs and go to the location that we were pretty sure where Connery lived at. We decided we would sit and wait, stake out the area and see if we could find Connery leaving a home or locating his car and seeing if a woman would at any time leave or enter the property. If the house I thought was the right one, it sat just off the corner of the block, just behind the pretty yellow house. But I just wasn't sure yet if this was the correct one, only time would tell. I had goggled Connery's name on the computer and it had given a general location but the address hadn't shown up on the Google so I still wasn't sure of it, but I knew we were close. I had planned on gluing my eyes to the front doors of the neighboring homes to see if anyone entered or left during the time Caleb and I would be sitting waiting for Connery to arrive or if a woman came or went, hopefully I would know soon.

I knew Caleb was getting tired I could see it in his eyes. It was taking longer than we had suspected to get prepared for this crazy venture. I hadn't spoken with Connery late in the afternoon as we usually did, so I wasn't sure if he would be going somewhere after work or even if he would be leaving on time. Since we hadn't left Caleb's house yet I was afraid Connery might have arrived at any one of the homes within the general location, prior to us arriving at the corner. If so, the waiting would do no good unless we decided to wait and see if he retreated from inside for some reason and caught him on his way out. I just wasn't sure about this idea anymore. What if Connery would see us, or what if we parked directly in front of his home, what would I do if he approached us for some insane reason? My stomach was in knots now.

A wife or a live in girlfriend, was there one? Had I just become another one of his women, his pets, and a part of his daily routine? I was determined to find out tonight!

It shouldn't take too long to make this discovery is what I told Caleb, but time was dragging and we still hadn't left yet, would we ever be able to leave?

Was Connery living with a woman or not? I was going insane. The waiting was stressful, and extremely nerve wrecking for me. It was still daylight, barely; the sun was going down fast. I hadn't wanted to be too obvious with this adventure, so dusk was the perfect time to head out. I was quite nervous about stalking Connery, so before we left for the rendezvous location, we each had a couple drinks, and I needed to loosen up a bit. Finally we left for the destination and after a while the wigs and costumes began to come off, slowly item by item. Caleb had taken a bottle of wine in the car and before too long he became too intoxicated to sit still any longer. I succumbed to the drink and soon realized the plans to catch Connery in his secret were not going to happen tonight. I disrobed of the costume, along with the long, hot blonde wig, and together we left the intersection perch. I drank the night away with Caleb for the most part and forgot about Connery for the time being. Never seeing a sign of him coming or going, nor of the car he drove.

I was saddened knowing the secrets I so desperately wanted to know wouldn't be revealed to me tonight. But eventually something would break, he would slip, a sign would show, maybe even someone I had mentioned his name to a few friends to see if any of them could have heard of him, possibly be friends of his as well, for the island was a small place and gossip traveled quickly and everyone knew everyone or was somehow connected to a mutual friend it seemed, so time would tell, this mysterious "Mr. Bond" would be exposed and the truth would be seen for what it was, nothing more to hide behind.

So I still knew nothing more of Connery than what I had known in the beginning but if Caleb was up for another time, staking out the approximate location of where I was pretty sure Connery lived we would have to make it happen and soon.

I was growing impatient with Connery, even though he had shared many things with me after just a short period of time, but there was still so much missing in the relationship. We never had gone out to dinner, with the exception of him riding with me to the local Taco House, on a lunch break, where he had loaned me a dollar to pay for my lunch. It had been just that a ride in the car to and from his work nothing more, then a kiss hello and a kiss goodbye when I dropped him back off. He had never taken me out on a date, to the movies, or a concert, we had never left the island or ever mentioned doing so from that very first comment he made to me about wanting to take me away for a weekend.

Some of my friends had begun to say I was stupid that he had to be married and I was just a woman he was using for sex. I refused to believe this, for when we were together it was like the Fourth of July, fireworks blaring out of control. If by some chance he was married, I could have cared less by this time, I was in this too deep to care. I would fight for his affection regardless of the situation. If I had to act the part of someone he didn't know when we passed in public or if I had to ignore him in such a way that wasn't too obvious then so be it. Because I needed him I needed his body, his attention, his inspiration, his sex. He already meant so much to me and I wasn't about to lose that not yet anyhow.

The next encounter I had with Connery, I flat out finally ask him if he had a wife.

"Are you married, you can tell me, it doesn't matter at all, just tell me"?

"No nothing like that, really!"

"Honestly, really all the pieces are there for that to be your secret your mystery the reason we don't have a normal dating life as most do."

"Well is it a girlfriend, or maybe even a boyfriend?"

"Oh God!!! No, none of that gay stuff!! It freaks me out, and why would any man that could have you, want to be gay?"

"Camille, you have such a gorgeous, voluptuous, obviously sexy body I could never imagine anyone not wanting to be with you, including me for the moment."

"I am definitely not what you want; I am not relationship material, for a variety of reasons."

"Who said I wanted you, Connery?"

"It's all just about sex, come on now, can't you tell that yet?"

"But why don't you want to be in a serious relationship? There are so many benefits from being with one person."

"No I totally disagree; no one should ever have to be monogamous, men and women were not made to be with just one person for a life time"

"What, that is ridiculous, Connery. A life with one can be a lifetime of joy, fun, fulfillment. Even you were married three times for whatever reason things didn't work out but you were faithful to the three when you were married to them, right?"

"I will not answer that, I am not going to discuss the whole reassurance thing and what happened to my marriages that is past and is of no concern to you as far as I can see it. If this is a matter that you can't seem to overlook or just get over, then we might as well be done, because for you all I am is a fun distraction at this time, but then, maybe not. If a fun distraction is all you want then we are good but don't ever try to tie me down it won't ever happen, I can promise you that."

So we had our first misunderstanding, finally, I knew it would happen eventually, it always does, no matter.

We resolved our differences and went our separate ways. I was somewhat distraught because now, I was afraid he wouldn't come back to me anymore. I couldn't bear the thought of losing him at this point.

I told him that I hated being his little amazing secret that had to be kept hidden away all the time? I was fine with being the "closet girlfriend" but at least let me know why it had to be that way. He had responded with stating, "That just part of the mystery, the way it has to be."

CHAPTER **13**

August was rapidly approaching. I had been seeing Connery, what seemed like a life time now, and I was totally smitten with him. He could do no wrong. The conversations we shared, the ideas we had, the rendezvous' we planned lying in my bed after making love, were always the highlight of the day. Sex was an awesome time we spent together, but now we could lie together and share so many things it was a comforting feeling. I could lay there for hours listening to him talk about any subject in the world; he seemed to know everything anyone would need to know, about anything. He was a great speaker and had a soft voice, and he knew how to hold my attention when talking. He had grown to trust me, I assumed or had he just tired of me always asking about his life. He had finally opened up and shared many life events with me how he had been with many women in his past, his jobs, his schooling, and his family. I was pleased to learn all the things I could about him. I felt like I knew him inside and out at times, all there was to know, but in reality I knew I would never know the real Connery Jackson he would always be that illusive butterfly.

Connery had talked about his younger years and how the women would line up to go out with him. He could have his pick of the litter. He had been a star football player in high school and in college. He could have been pro if he would have desired to be but his life had taken a different direction and football took second seat. He had even shown me photographs of him during those years. He had been an extremely good looking young man. I could understand why all the girls lined up to go out with him even in those days. If he was sexually active in his younger years as he was now, my mind could only imagine how many women he could have been with. Had he ever thought to keep count for his own benefit?

He had talked about how he had become involved with a somewhat older set of friends, both men and women. This group he classified as swingers, couples that traded spouses, or dates at a particular location when they met to have sex. He was what a lot of young men his age considered lucky for lack of no other word, for he could have sex with as many women as he was capable of performing for on any one of these given "date" night events. He had learned from these older women what a woman needed when it came to sex, how to touch them, where to kiss them, when to use more pressure, more force with his body, be more gentle, softer, less intense. This would be the experiences that would make him what he had become today, a worldly man, and extremely knowledgeable when it came to having sex with not just one woman in particular, but with any woman. He had learned by trial and process of elimination, the dos and don'ts of sexual acts. Something most men never in a lifetime had an opportunity to do. He had learned how to be a Gentleman.

He had learned well, because he knew how to fuck me! He had made me climax eighteen times once. We had counted each and everyone one of them together! My body would convulsive repeatedly as he touched the right spots, kissed me the right way. Once he had sucked my toes one by one on each foot. I never even knew he had never placed his rock hard cock inside me because the toe sucking had been all it took to make me squeal with climatic chirps as he softly sucked each toe one by one, until I was completely spent. I had never had my toes sucked before and it was something I enjoyed more than words could even explain. How many other places on my body could he kiss, suckle, lick, or bite that had never been touched or used as a sexual pleasure, we would have to find out together.

Even though I adored Connery so much more than any of the other men I had dated and was able to be with him as often as we desired to be together, there still was Franklin, the second man I met and dated since I had gotten on the dating site.

Franklin could be the marrying type in time, if I could hold on to him long enough, but I still felt the need to date others besides just him and Connery. So I dated all that I could and enjoyed every minute of my time with each man I was with.

Never realizing the impact Connery would have on my life. Nor how the fact that Franklin's life and my mine were so parallel. These two, would be the two men that I would share my body with and grow to have undeniable admiration and affection for, but in such different capacities, a capacity I never knew a heart could have. Would they feel the same way about me? Or was it just about sex?

Connery mentioned to me on one occasion that a three way might be fun. He had asked if I knew of a man that could be a part of our little rendezvous one day. I had told him that Franklin might be interested in playing along but that I would have to ask and then get back with him.

Franklin and Connery both, together just the thought of that made me have an orgasm. What would that be like? Connery was so awesome when it came to penetration and foreplay and Franklin was fabulous at oral sex. I might pass out with the actions of both going at me at the same time. A literal death by fucking, could that really happen? I could just see the local newspaper headlines "Middle aged woman dies during three way sex!"

I knew Connery was serious about this inquiry so I made it a point to question Franklin how he felt about things of that nature. Franklin, well let's just say, he was all for it!

For me it would be nothing new, for I had been in a three way on several occasions. A few of those times were with William. William's three ways consisted of me and two men, usually one being William, but not always.

William had decided after all those years of marriage that he preferred to watch me with other men at times. Yes, at first I was astounded by this announcement, for there had never been an inkling of an idea that he had ever wanted to include anyone else in our sex acts, while we were together. We had very healthy sexual habits for a married couple but in the last few years I had noticed things were changing but I chalked it up as a mid-life crisis, those things men and women both seem to go through.

After I had been on a short trip out of town alone and so excited to be back home and be with him he had refused to kiss me much less make love to me, in fact he told me he was not even going to stay home with me that night, he was leaving an going to the weekend home, the one I now resided in, alone in Galveston.

I cried so hard, I had missed him so much and so wanted to be with him, but agreed finally to let him go, not knowing what was going on in his mind but I knew arguing was not going to get me anywhere. He had left me alone so I unpacked, made some dinner and rested for a while then finally went to bed wondering what had I done, what was wrong. No matter what it was I knew William well enough to know he would eventually tell me and I knew it would be something I had done, or not done. That's just the way it always seemed to go, never anything he did or said, always me.

The next morning I woke up early and another major event took place, something that wasn't needed at this time.

I was notified that my job was playing out in ninety days, this rocked my world. With the emotions of a husband not wanting to be with me after a two week absence and now no job, I felt as if my life was ending and I had no idea why. I decided I needed to call William, tell him about the job, hoping he would answer the phone. I hesitated at first, wondering if that was the right thing to do, but I needed him now, I needed his shoulder to lean on, to cry on, and besides he should have been there for me anyhow. I dialed the number, he answered immediately, thank goodness for when I heard his voice I lost complete control of myself. I burst into tears and couldn't stop. He finally was able to tell me that he was almost home that he was less than ten minutes from me and he would be there to take care of me. He tried to reassure me that everything would be alright, but it wasn't and it wouldn't be. The income I was bringing home was the income that was paying for the weekend home in Galveston, and all I could think of was how would we pay for it? I knew that we would probably have to sell it, and that literally made me sick to my stomach.

Shortly William arrived home; he took me in his arms and consoled me like a husband should do. I felt somewhat better, but deep inside I was coming apart. We stood at the entryway and talked, and cried together. Slowly we made our way to the kitchen area where I was finally able to stop the sobbing tears, and relax for a second. I sat on the bench at the dining table and William leaned up against the cabinets. We stared at space silently for a few minutes then I ask him why had he left me why had he just had to leave the very night I had come home, did he not miss me, not want to be with me? I was hurt deeply and I let him know that. He agreed with me that he shouldn't have gone but then he looked me in the eyes and said, Camille there is something I need to tell you and it's not going to be easy so please listen without interruption because this is important and I don't want you to jump to any conclusions, so please hear what I have to say. Of course with this kind of statement that made the hair on my arms stand at attention. My mind was going crazy and my heart was breaking for I could tell in his tone that this was not going to be good, no matter what it was. I immediately thought he had maybe lost his job, or maybe one of the kids had been hurt, or one of our parents had passed, something of this nature, whatever it was he had to tell me. He had my full attention.

He began to speak to tell me how much he loved me, how much I meant to him, how much he had missed me, but, while I was gone he had been with someone else. I knew it! He had been having an affair, probably with one of those girls from the gym that he just wasn't ever able to stay away from, for any reason. I hated that gym with a passion. Now it all made sense to me, finally. But no, I wasn't hearing him correctly, he was telling me he had left me the day before because he had made his mind up that he was going to commit suicide, so that he would never have to explain to me who he really was and had been all those years we had been together. My ears were hearing different words, but as he spoke of his time spent in Galveston while I was away, that it hadn't been with a woman, but on the contrary he had spent the entire two weeks with a man, a man that we were both acquainted with, a gay man at that. I know my eyes froze in a blank stare, I remember as though I was in a dream and couldn't move, couldn't speak just frozen in time. As he continued to talk, he told me he had been sexually involved with this man, but that penetration had not happened but oral sex and fondling had. How could this be? He had been a deacon in the church, a leader in the community, a godly man most would say. I was hearing these words coming from his mouth but my heart and mind would not allow me to believe a word of it. He began to cry, weeping out of control. I never moved to console him; I just sat there on the bench waiting for his next words. When he would stop crying, he would tell me how much he loved me over and over again, and that the lifestyle he had the past two weeks were not what he wanted, he wanted me and only me. He was sorry for what had happened but begged me please not to leave him for this was a onetime indiscretion and he would never allow it to happen again, ever.

Shocked as any woman and wife would be, all I wanted to do was to run, get out of there as fast as I could. To be alone to think and consume the conversation, digest it, if possible. He finished talking, wanting to hold me. My first thought was to not allow him to touch me, but I gave in, at first, I shared with him that I had many questions and I would demand answers, and the truth before I could make my decision what I should do regarding us, for the time being. But immediately I blurted out "Absolutely no more sex between the two of us for an undeterminable amount of time, or if ever again".

The expression on his face didn't change for I imagined he had expected a comment of that nature from me regardless of how our marriage would end up, together or apart. This would take time to heal if it could.

CHAPTER 14

William and I had decided to give our marriage a chance, well I had decided to! He would have to prove to me that he wanted no part of a gay relationship and that no other person, man or woman would ever come between us. He had deceived me all those years. Had he always been gay, had thoughts of being with a man. Why had he married me? Was it to hide his true feelings, to prevent events of which society would have treated him during those years? I had just been a front for him to make him look like everyone thought he should look like? GOD only knew. I had made up my mind to try to make our marriage work for the thought of having to start over at my age wasn't something I wanted to consider. I had no career, no college, never been with another man. I had been a stay at home wife and mother most of our years together and was completely terrified of the thought that if this marriage didn't stay together that I would be alone, lost, having nothing to rely on for income, how would I survive this world alone?

In our agreement to give it one last shot, William had asked me to never leave him alone again, never allow him to go anywhere without me. That could be easy enough but if his desires were stronger than what he let on, then my work would be cut out for me.

I allowed him to continue to sleep in the same bed but we never touched, never kissed, and absolutely never had any sexual connections at all.

Finally, a few weeks later, he approached me with an option that blew me away; he wanted to have an open marriage. He wanted to be able to come and go without questions, to stay out all night or nights which ever occurred. He wanted me to play along with him be the woman he would at times want to include in a three way, with him and one of his gay lovers. I know my facial expression must have said it all, for I just sat there blown away, again at a statement of this nature coming from his mouth. What was happening to our marriage? Should I just get out while I could with only the damage done to me at this point? I didn't know what to do, what to say, how to respond to his suggestions. Frozen in time is how I felt. This was the worst nightmare I had ever had and I wanted to wake up from this unknown element and fast.

I had a difficult time understanding his words; even though I heard them clearly I did not understand where this was all coming from. We had both been seeing therapists, separately of course and I felt like we were making progress. Boy was I wrong, for he had changed his mind and though he wasn't sure he wanted to leave me he did know he wanted to be "free" so to speak to live his life as he chose, but he wanted me to be a part of it still as well. I fought, battled within on how to deal with this, but fear of loneliness and insecurity won out. I agreed to play along with his wishes, under one condition that I as well could date, see other men with no questioning from him, no repercussions what so ever. For if he was going to be out fucking men, then so could I!

And with that a new era began in our so called marriage, a marriage that wasn't going to last long I was sure of, because of my upbringing and religious beliefs, and the fear that GOD was about to strike me dead at any moment for involving myself in acts that I knew were not what a wife, should be partaking of with her husband, if I could even call him a husband anymore.

So we starting going out, taking his "friends" along with us. We frequented the gay bars, started drinking a lot, for me it was the only way I was able to survive this abominable situation I had to live through. Alcohol was my savior during this time, it allowed me to party, do things I would have never done, but most of all it allowed me to forget what happened on these nights out. It gave me the strength, sorry to say to continue on as a wife of a now predominately gay husband, a husband that was demanding many things of me. William had often brought men home with us. Thank goodness I was drunk out of my mind most of the time, because we would have sex, I would perform blow jobs on these men, all while William watched, sometimes he even took pictures of the acts, why was he doing this? Did he have a specific reason, but the alcohol was to strong, I didn't have the strength to fight off the camera, or the men. I did what I thought I needed to do, to keep my husband, to survive. A mistake I would regret for the rest of my life

So when Connery mentioned a three way it didn't faze me one bit. But would Franklin really want to be a part of that for some reason I just didn't think he would come through. Besides, I didn't know if I really would want the two of them to meet under those circumstances.

CHAPTER 15

Franklin and I had met on a different dating site than I had met Michael or Connery on. Franklin was a tall man at least six foot four and was large, but portioned well. He had a shaved head, only peach fuzz, which made his head soft to the touch. He sported a mustache, but no beard. In his profile picture he had on a cowboy hat, boots, jeans and a Texas style belt buckle. He was leaning up against a pickup truck, that was most likely his, but it didn't matter to me if it wasn't. His pose was stern, his arms were crossed, no smile on his face. But there was something about his look that had reminded me of someone, someone that had meant a lot in my life and the expression he wore was like my grandfather had been reincarnated, for his eyes looked right through Franklin's eyes. When I looked at Franklin's picture all I could see was genuine kindness, a hidden soft side that he probably never allowed anyone to see, except on accident.

We exchanged phone numbers and scheduled a call. He was going to call me, unusual for most it had seemed these days for the women were expected to call the men if they were interested at all.

The phone rang, it was him. We had the usual introductions and then he brought the subject up that he had been in law enforcement, was looking to get out as soon as he could, and he had also just moved to the area from up East. He told me his wife of twenty nine years had packed his bags and one evening when he came home from work there they were, all lined up at the front door. She told him she didn't love him anymore, and wanted him out that night. Shocked by this with no other explanation at the time, what else could he do except go. They would later sit down and do what needed to be done, divorce!

Franklin had mentioned he liked Tequila and the minute he said that, I knew we could have lots of fun together, for Patron was my drink of choice. So I made a bet with him that I could out shoot him shot for shot if he wanted to meet up and bring his best Tequila shot glasses with him! He had agreed. We planned a date to meet at my house and have a few shots and just take the evening from there. I knew, after the first date just a few days before with Michael, that I should be prepared for anything, and anything meant sex! I was comfortable with Franklin from just the phone calls, so I was really looking forward to meeting this Cowboy!

He was coming over on Saturday night after he had slept the afternoon; he was working graveyards and would need to sleep some before he drove down to the island. He lived about forty-five minutes from my place, so not too far, to come on occasions if it came to that, and not too close to be here all the time either.

Considering this would be my second man I had met on a dating site and my second date in years, this one would be different from the one with Michael, for Franklin and I were meeting at my house and would take the night from there, but what if we started drinking and couldn't drive what would he do then? I prepared the back bedroom for possible company just to be safe. Laughing on the inside for I knew if we hit it off there was no way he would be sleeping in the back bedroom but would be right there beside me in my big four poster king bed that held only me for the last year. The thought of having a man sleeping with me, actually sleeping with me was a good feeling.

Franklin showed up Saturday right on time. He had worn jeans, and a nice button down shirt with short sleeves, comfortable clothes, nothing binding or stiff. He had not worn a cowboy hat but instead had on a baseball cap. He was tall, with tanned forearms, soft fuzzy head, freshly shaven face and trimmed mustache. He had a deep voice but when he laughed his belly rolled. His laughter came from deep down, and was not pretentious but real. He wore wire rimmed glasses and a big old ring on his finger.

We sat side by side on my sofa and visited for a bit then I broke out the Tequila. I offered him Patron but he said he preferred Jose Cuervo if I had that brand. Really, Cuervo was for making drinks with, and wasn't smooth like Patron for shooting. But he again declined the Patron and so I brought him a bottle of Cuervo that had been given to William and me as a gift from a trip to Mexico from some friends. So the night began with shots of Tequila. As I had predicted I had out shot him but I really believed he could go on for a while but didn't want to get so drunk that we couldn't even carry on a conversation. Franklin was funny he made me laugh. I felt so comfortable around him already! Was I just lonely and any man would be able to make me so at ease? Were all men like, Franklin, Michael, and Connery? This was almost too easy.

We talked about our lives, our children, and strange enough he talked a lot about his soon to be x wife. He shared with me the story of their relationship and some of the highlights of their life together. He missed her dearly, and regretted all the things he had done wrong over the years that had climaxed into a separation and most likely a divorce, this would be divorce number three for him as well, seemingly all three of these men, Michael, Connery and now Franklin all had been married three times. Was number four the magic number or number three the time to stop?

I had a great time with Franklin and when the night became late we started kissing, touching each other and before long we were in the bed in heated sexual acts. Franklin was loose, not as suave as Connery but good. He made me laugh, do things I had never thought of doing and we ended the evening holding each other tight until the morning light woke us. He had to leave for he had to be at work that evening again but did tell me he would be back and he had a great time, as did I. I wanted Franklin, for some reason and I realized this from the very first date we ever had. This meeting would continue on for four years and having worlds of fun together, sharing, the good times and the bad times of our past, our children, our wants and wishes, I was falling in love with this man, and falling hard! I wanted to be his wife his magic number four.

CHAPTER 16

Connery was patient, never in a hurry when it came to sex, though he never gave me more than an hour or two at the most at any given time, with the exception of the holiday weekend in September 2010.

I had accepted a date with a man for Labor Day weekend, a new guy. We were to meet and go for dinner on Monday afternoon, but before Monday came I knew I wasn't up for it. The thought of spending my first holiday without William was almost too much for me to bear at the moment. So I had canceled the date and decided to stay at home and drown in my sadness and depression once again. The day had been decent enough but night time had approached quickly and I was feeling lonely and sad. I knew William would have gone to the lake having tons of fun with all the family drinking and telling all sorts of stories as the night crept into the wee morning hours. We would have been there together sitting around the campfires if we would have still been together but in August the divorce had come final and now I was all alone and William was with someone else.

As the late evening got even later I had begun to drink a bottle of wine, wine always made me drunk fast especially on an empty stomach. Since the dinner date had been canceled I had just forgotten about eating and now I was paying the price. I was getting drunk fast and had even begun taking shots all alone. Sleep was nowhere in my thoughts so I decided to get on the computer and see if any of my friends were on line at that late night hour. Not expecting anyone to be at home much less on the computer, but as I glanced down towards the messenger there he was! Connery was on line at one in the morning. Why I wondered, but I had never been on the computer that time of night either so maybe he was on there this late often? He saw me and messaged me. I was delighted to know he had seen me and wanted to chat.

He asked me what I was doing and I told him of the canceled date and the sadness I was feeling for the loss of William and the first holiday after the divorce. I told him I was drinking wine and feeling pretty good at the moment and sure would love for him to come over if he was available. Knowing that if he said no, or made some excuse then I would know he was in a relationship for what man, husband, boyfriend, lover, whatever you want to call them, would be able to just get up and leave at 1 am to rendezvous with a woman to have sex?

He told me how he hated wine and never drank the stuff because who in their right mind would want to drink sour grape juice and for what reason, to have an aching head the next day.

We chatted on line for a bit about nothing really and then I just ask, if he could come over? To my astonishment he said yeah, he could be there in about thirty minutes. I couldn't believe my eyes! Was he really coming over on a holiday night to see me? This was the answer to the mystery I wasn't able to solve until now, this was the first time I completely believed he was unattached. If he was able to come over and maybe spend the night with me and we could wake together holding each other in our arms after a unbelievable evening of the most remarkable sex I could have ever imagined of having. Was I dreaming? I had to read the words again.

I replied to him, well I will give you thirty minutes so get going! I asked him why he needed thirty minutes and his reply was he had to get his mother to sleep first. He had already told me that his parents lived with him so that comment was believable enough and it made since. He had told me on one occasion that his mother was bipolar and had always seemed to have her days and nights confused for as long as he could remember. So I took his statement for what it was worth. He had typed stating, that she didn't ever go to bed before two am almost but he was trying his best to get her down as fast as possible so he could come on over.

I told him I would have a drink ready for him when he got here . . . a blow job shot!

He laughed and remarked that he would prefer the blow job over the shot!

So thirty minutes . . . I started timing him and it was almost thirty minutes and he still wasn't here, and was still on line.

I questioned him what's taking so long? He would reply with some pathetic excuse but it didn't really matter because if he was really coming I would surely be in heaven soon enough for having sex with Connery was the most wonderful thing in my world.

A second time I messaged him, it's been forty-five minutes now! Are you coming or not?

He replied yes I am walking out right now will be there if less than five minutes.

So he showed up just like he said he would, there he was standing at my front door at two am in the morning in a pair of shorts, t-shirt and flip flops. I had never seen him dressed in anything other than his work clothes up until now. He was so handsome, GOD I wanted him so bad, there were no words to describe that feeling I was having that very moment. He was there and I was ready and willing to do anything he asked of me.

He entered and I locked the doors behind him. We stood momentarily kissing in the living room and then slowly made our way to the bedroom where he quickly removed his shorts, and t-shirt. He sprawled across my huge four poster bed laying side to side vs. head to foot and just before he laid his head down I offered him that blow job shot I had prepared for him sitting right there on the bedside table. To my unbelief he accepted it and swallowed it all in one gulp. He then looked at me with a yearning glance and I in my drunken stupor followed his eyes down to his cock, which was fully erect and waiting for my mouth to take it in and lavish it with my tongue till his body ached with joyful agonizing pain and he fully relieved himself and ejaculated with all the power stowed up inside him.

As my mouth approached his cock I smelled the odor of sex. Strange, I thought why would he been smelling of sex and here to have sex with me. So my thoughts, drunken though they were, wandered again, was he just a player, or could he possibly have had sex with a wife, a girlfriend, and now wanted sex with me? Connery was something else! I was just drunk enough to not care if his dick had been inside some other woman prior to coming to my house so I leaned down and suckled his hard dick with all my being and thought nothing more about the scent of some other woman's sex on his cock in my mouth.

We played like this for a while and then I lied down on the bed and he took me in his mouth. I was in the state of delirium almost drunk with wine and drunk with him having come to me in the middle of the night to be with me to make love to me. What more could I have wanted at the moment. Connery was my geographically convenient living sex toy that was for sure! Eventually we fucked with a precision and determination like no other time before. I climaxed repeatedly as he always made me do. He had a knack for making that happen often, unlike anyone else I had been with except Franklin.

After sex we lied there together dozing off and on and I ask him to stay the night. He had mumbled something that I didn't understand and I passed it off as just what it was a mumble. I ask again and he said he couldn't stay till morning because he would have to be there when his mother woke up because she would wander off. That was hard for me to understand but I was happy that he had been able to come to me, and cum! He did stay much longer than the lunch sex and after work sex encounters we were so accustomed to having, which was a milestone for he had never come over in the night time, never stayed with me like this, never drank with me, never not once, so this again made me realize he couldn't have had a wife at home for what wife would have had sex with her husband and then let him leave the house at two a.m. and stay gone until the wee hours of the morning and never questioned his were about. No woman in her right mind would have ever allowed this to happen so for now I was convinced he was single for the moment.

Finally he rose up after dozing for a short time and said he needed to leave. I didn't question him or ask him to stay again, but rejoiced in the fact that he had come over and made me a very happy woman. I had not been alone on the first holiday after my divorce, but had spent a least a small portion of it now with Connery having awesome sex and indulging myself in wine. How and what would I think tomorrow?

I walked Connery to the front door and there he slipped back on his clothes with the door wide open for anyone to see if they looked, not caring that if they did they would only see two people naked in the moonlight kissing goodbye for the night and going on about their separate ways. He dressed and left in the twinkling of an eye.

Morning came and after I got over the headache and the unsurpassable thought that Connery had just been there, the thought of the scent of sex being on him upon his arrival to my house just hours earlier, made me think twice about where could that have come from? I was baffled again of his mysteriousness and couldn't seem to shake the feeling again of there being someone who had him by the apron strings, someone he was committed to but had no problems cheating on the side as well. How ignorant could this woman be, to not know that her man was seeing another woman, possibly more than one? I couldn't imagine being her.

CHAPTER 17

Monday had come and gone. It had been exciting, depressing, sad, lonesome, fulfilling and comforting all in one. I had survived the first holiday without William and had a surprising unexpected time with Connery. What would September bring me? I could hardly wait to see what the future was holding in store for me.

William had called and said he needed to come by and see me; it was a little unusual that he would be demanding a visit in the middle of a holiday week I thought. Had I been wrong about him being at the lake? Obliviously he was here if he wanted to come by. So I agreed to see him not really wanting to, especially when he told me Clark would be coming with him when he came. Clark was Williams lover the one I had caught him with, I wasn't wanting to ever see his face again as long as I lived but I realized that would never happen, if I was to do the best that I could to keep some kind of semblance of caring in our family for the children and our grandson.

It would be difficult for me to see the two of them together, here in what was our house, now mine, but I would have to make the best of it. I was strong and knew I could survive this if I really wanted to.

So William and Clark arrived later in the afternoon on Tuesday the first Tuesday in September 2010. They hadn't knocked or announced their arrival but had just come on in as if nothing had ever changed in our lives, as if we were still husband and wife, and Clark just one of our gay friends. I had been in the bedroom putting away clothes and they just came on in, made their selves at home, chitchatting about nothing.

When I was done and about to exit the bedroom, William mentioned something about an object there he saw on the dresser and started a peculiar conversation, like he was wasting time, then Clark appeared in the door way as well. Little did I know, what the next few minutes would hold for me, not in my innermost imagination would I have ever thought what was about to happen happened and that William, the man I had loved and still loved, would stand by and watch this horrible ordeal evolve before his very eyes.

CHAPTER 18

William and I had been friends with many people in the gay community, I had never been insensitive, or belittling towards any of them, but I had also never expected my husband to be gay. Some of these friends were men he had been seeing, and one in particular we had been friendlier with than others, for some reason, but we had connected with him. We later found out that he too was married had children but had come out of the closet somewhere within the last few years and his wife and accepted him and let him live the life he wanted but had chosen to stay married to him for financial reasons.

This man, Clark Wilson had his sights set on William from the beginning I would realize this too late, after it was all said and done. If I had known this in the beginning I would have broken off the friendship as fast as a speeding bullet, but I hadn't. Clark, the friend, had been on the prowl trying man after man in search of finding a gay lover that had money someone he could take as his own and live off his lovers income and someone to feel a void in his life and support him in his career as a drag queen. William would end up being the one! But in the meantime, William, Clark and I played, played the games of the open life style. Even though I never had intercourse with Clark, thank goodness, there were many things we did together, the three of us that

I have regretted since and would regret throughout eternity. The past was past, the damage was done.

Clark and William eventually moved in together, as a gay couple, leaving me to fend for myself. I soon found out Clark had fed William many lies and had focused his aim on me, to hurt me in ways I had never been hurt before. Shortly after we agreed to separate and I had finally realized this gay three way life style was nowhere near what I wanted for my life, and I'd be damned if I was going to live the rest of my life like that. I was angry now, hurt beyond words, and didn't care what William was doing or with who for that matter, he would have to deal with his decisions in the end as would I, but I knew I wanted out and out I was getting, but not before Clark made sure I was damaged goods.

So here they were together, again this time as a couple, William and Clark to see me at the Galveston house, for what reason I was not quite sure, but I had agreed that they could stop by.

This day an event would take place that would be the one thing I would never be able to forgive William for, throughout the rest of my life. He would pay for his actions throughout eternity.

On this visit he and Clark, had set up with another man, a man whom had been in our home once before during the time we were together and trying to make the marriage work. He was to wait for the instructions of what they wanted him to do. In these instructions he'd been told to meet them at the Galveston house about the same time that Clark and William would be arriving. Later I would find out that he had been instructed to wait outside and they would call for him when ready, to make his entrance into the house and things would go from there.

I had just walked across the bedroom when William and his lover came in, we had a few unpleasant words, and I went on about the things I was doing there in the bedroom. While William was talking to me about something there on the dresser, I could tell he was upset, angry but I wasn't interested in knowing why and wasn't paying him much attention and this exasperated him he demanded my attention. I turned to look him in the eye and at that very moment Clark and now another man, Ricky was his name, approached the bedroom door. Ricky moved forward in front of Clark and even William, he entered the room and William and Clark stepped back a few steps. I still wasn't paying much attention, just thinking what was this Ricky guy doing here, was he gay as well? He had been with a girlfriend, when we had met the first and only time we had ever seen each other. Ricky just stood there momentarily.

William began to raise his voice telling me he and Clark had brought me a gift, a surprise, something they knew I desperately needed and it was Ricky! They had brought him to rape me, but in their minds they had brought Ricky to have sex with me. They both remembered too well the last time I had sex, as far as they were aware of, for it had been a while. They both had been there on that last time, for William and I were in the mist of sex when Clark walked in on us, as he had been allowed to do per William, no matter how I felt, and had climbed up on the bed and was behind William at the time, telling me not to worry all he was doing was putting pressure on William's backside, helping him push deeper inside me, but in reality, just at the moment he had completed saying those very words, William had a dreadful, painful expression come across his face and I knew that Clark had inserted himself into Williams ass, even while William was still inside me. He had not climaxed yet but with this event, I shoved William off of me and he never completed the act, and this would be the last time William and I would ever have sex together for the rest of our lives as far as I was concerned, and to know that Clark had been a part of that would add to the horrifying memory of sex with the man I had loved for so many years, nothing would ever be able to remove that feeling that moment in time for me, ever!

And, now here William standing in the bedroom door way was now making jokes of how much I loved sex and probably had missed it so much and probably was too big of a chicken to just go out and fuck just anyone so they had brought Ricky there to supply and meet my need. William and Clark blocked the doorway with their bodies as I fought to free myself from the bedroom. Ricky was undressed, standing naked; pulling me with his strong muscular arms towards the bed, I screamed out no please don't do this to me, please! Please, NO!

I was fighting a losing battle my body was weak and I had nothing to fight with to free myself from the three men. Ricky threw me onto the bed and ripped my clothes off of my body and fucked me using his, huge muscular arms to pen me down, all while William and Clark still standing at the door, enjoying every moment of this torture as they watched with grins and snickering as I succumbed to this man's attack on my body as well as my soul, my very being was being mutilated by this man, but more so, the fact that William standing there taking sport and delight in the fact that I was being forcefully raped at his command no less, made me oblivious to the painful act that was taking place inside my body, who was William now? How could he allow this to happen?

As I lie there, my mind not knowing where to place my thoughts, I wondered had I allowed this to happen, I hadn't fought hard enough, I was actually being raped and my X husband was standing there watching, not helping me not protecting me as a husband would, but in fact he was the instigator of the entire set up and just stood there and watched while some strange man sexually ravaged me in what used to be our bed.

Before Ricky was finished with me, William and Clark left the house, they had accomplished what they had set out to accomplish and there was no need for them to be there any longer. I had given in and they had just left me there, not knowing what else this man would do with me. Once Ricky had finally cum, he rammed his swollen cock in my mouth and forced me to have oral sex with him, I was crying, begging him to please just leave he had gotten what he came for and there was no need to pursue oral sex, but he didn't go until he was done with me. He left without a word, never looking back, never wondering what I might do if he turned his back on me, for all he knew I might have a hand gun in the side table, a knife, but I hadn't and he wasn't afraid of something that he was pretty sure wouldn't take place. He left and I lie there sobbing, wondering why this had happened and why William had allowed it, it had to be Clark and at this point I realized William, really and finally was not mine anymore, if he had ever been.

I had completely lost him to the world, a world that he had embraced behind my back, a world that had given him the things that he had so desired and had kept hidden all those many years. It was over, my life had changed. I would move on from here to a better place. Let him go! Just let him go, is all I kept telling myself. Let him go!

CHAPTER 19

During the time between the rape, the separation, the divorce, and the time William and I tried to make things work, and obviously they hadn't, I had decided to try the dating sites and see what it was like to date, and with this decision many things in my life changed drastically but it got me away from the likes of Clark and William and took me to a place of real men, real sex, and a deception I had heard about but never had experienced it for myself.

Now after meeting Connery with his mysterious ways, I once again thought of the deception men used on women, the lies they told, the games they played. All I had wanted was to find a man to love and someone to love me back but Connery wasn't that man. I knew it already even from the beginning when he deceived me with the picture on the dating site that wasn't a real picture of him but of some unknown man, a man that I had fallen for, had a strong desire to meet, to be with only wanting to hope that one day I might have a man like Connery as my own, to take the place of William, but it didn't look like it would ever happen.

There had been Michael, the photographer, Franklin, the law enforcer, Jimmy, the wood floor owner, Presley, the Robert Redford look alike, so many men. Some deserving of a good woman I imagined but I wasn't ready to stop with these first few. I would continue on dating until there were at least thirty before meeting Connery.

Michael and Franklin both, I saw often, especially Franklin. Michael had started dating Lisa, another woman he met on the dating site and he was falling for her, but in time she would be the one that would deceive him. Amidst the sex, and meeting men on the dating site deception was always the one thing that amazed me the most. Everyone was playing a game of some sort. No one seemed to care about anything except deceiving the other one way or the other.

The deception of men and women was so incomprehensible at times. How and why, would a person choose to be someone they weren't, unless they had something to hide? Most of them did have something to hide, and from what I had seen it was generally a husband or a wife. Waiting at home, not knowing the infidelity of their spouse and the dating site games they played to obtain sex from others.

September was fading fast, Michael was involved with Lisa full time, and Franklin who I so would have enjoyed seeing a lot more was working everyday he could, and just didn't have the time to make it down to see me as much as I would have liked, so I started dating more again. I met Adam on the Fishing for Love date site, the same site I had met Connery on. He was an engineer with the local space group and had only been married once; he loved his dogs and treated them as if they were his children, not a bad habit in reality. He lived about an hour drive from me but had nothing else to do on the weekends except dog shows which he attended frequently with the kennel club where he had purchased his beloved pets and where he kenneled them when he left town. The owner had been a young Asian woman that he had spoken of often in a friendly sort of way and blatantly noted during one conversation that he would never have anything sexual to do with her because she was a real pain in the ass! What that meant I had no idea at the moment.

Adam was as far from the look of a man that I liked as the North Pole was from the South, but he had money and enjoyed going out, a change of pace for me vs. just meeting to have sex.

Adam was nice, but shy and timid in a sweet way. He was smaller in statue than any of the other men I had dated by this time. His face was always clean shaven and irritated me every time we were together. The one reason I preferred men with beards over those without.

Our first date together we had planned on eating at the Italian Restaurant on the Strand and then maybe, going for drinks at a bar that over looked the water. And if I played my cards right we might make it back to my house afterwards to see how good he was at sex if he was lucky.

Adam was not extremely handsome in fact he was nothing at all like what I had been used to or had even desired to be with but he was innocent and this presented somewhat of a challenge to me. A seemingly innocent man in today's society was not something a woman came across very often anymore as far as I had seen. So it was invigorating to be with him, a pleasant change.

He had a short haircut and was balding badly on the crown of his head. He must have been no taller than me and had a reddish complexion. He wore glasses at all times and had a squeaky voice. He did have a nice smile and when he smiled it was almost like he was flashing a neon bill board stating, that he hadn't been laid in years! Well we would end that soon enough I imagined.

After dinner and a couple drinks we came back to my house made our way to the sofa and began kissing. He was uncomfortable I could tell. Had it been ages since he had even kissed a woman? We necked and then his hands started groping my crotch area and before long he had his hands in my panties and was rubbing me causing a slight wetting sensation. This was causing him to get hard and with each rub he became like a rabid animal doing everything within his power to overtake his prey. Soon he raised his body and sat in my lap and pulled the spaghetti strap of my dress off my shoulder and began tugging at my nipple with his mouth. He wanted me and wanted me bad. I was playing with his emotions and wasn't sure if I wanted to allow him to have me sexually or not. We kissed and undressed before long and I finally gave in and ask him to move to the bed so if we were going to fuck we would at least be comfortable. I pulled the bronze duvet cover back and the soft pink sheets revealed underneath were cool to the touch and inviting as we lay there together. He reached in his pocket, took out a handful of condoms and put one on his long lean dick, even his genitals were unusual, and unlike the large long girth ones I'd been having the delight in seeing the past months. He finally got the condom on and mounted me in the typical missionary style position doing everything he could to get his skinny dick inside me before it blasted its wad all over the place.

Adam was frustrated and I just wanted to laugh it was like it was his first time ever. He couldn't get in the right position, couldn't get the condom to stay up, he was in a hurry for some strange reason and then I found out why. Suddenly he blew it, the sperm went everywhere, he winced in pain but I felt sure it was a good pain at least I hoped so. He immediately began to apologize for not making it inside me before he came and I couldn't hold it any longer I burst out laughing. He didn't know how to take that but I made it easy for him, and told him, how was he to know that I loved it when a man ejaculated on my belly and breasts, that it was fine, that penetration wasn't necessary and I was enjoying the moment. All I could think was what a dork!

He began talking telling me it had been ages and he was so sorry he was embarrassed even that he hadn't been able to control his wad long enough to insert himself into my now sticky vaginal opening. I was miserable but, had enjoyed our time together. At the moment I didn't care if we saw each other again or not. Sex was not that good, obviously, and besides I still had Connery for good sex any day of the week when I so desired, so Adam was just a tryst a thing, a toy to play with for a while, if he wanted to hang around. So Adam joined the long list of men that I met on occasion to have sexual encounters with. Now I was playing the deceiving game, when had the game turned and put me in this position?

Little did I realize that night that Adam and I would end up dating until February, we would go out on Valentines weekend, do Tequila shots at the Tequila bar in town and after he brought me home that night we made love on the sofa. When he left a little after three a.m. that would be the last time I would ever see him again until almost a year later. I had begun to fall for Adam, but he had no idea, I had never let on that my feelings were becoming more than just a casual thing but in the end things happen for a reason, so I was glad I had never shared those thoughts with him. To have lost him so fast would have been more devastating than it was. I had begun to even think maybe I could live with him, give it a go, if the subject ever came up. He had money, a good job, similar interests as me and he loved dogs. But things turned out differently and I was okay with it in the end.

After Adam and during the months that followed our first date, since we had never spoken of our relationship being exclusive I dated many other men from the dating sites. In fact I stepped up the pace and got back into the routine of dating two or three different men on any given weekend, always having Connery there during the week and Franklin almost every other week or weekend depending on his work schedule. So I wasn't going without if anything I was getting sex more often now, than I had in the summer months when Connery and I had been meeting so many times a day and almost every day of the week.

Adam was history and it was time to move one.

Anthony came next he was very young; he had a fourteen year old son at home that lived with him. He lived further than most men I had dated. To get to the island he had to come across the ferry every trip. That sometimes would take up to or longer than an hour one way. He was dark, olive skinned with a partial bald head but the hair that remained was dark no gray in site. He sported the beard in form of a goatee and had the mustache to match. He was slightly overweight but was just a living doll.

He'd hurt his knee recently and just completed a second surgery on it shortly before we met. So sex with him would be interesting. Would he be able to carry his own weight when it came to getting it on with me, if it got that far? We had many conversations on the phone in the evenings when he got home from work, we talked about our dreams and the places we had always wanted to visit. Both of us had dreamed of going to Africa at least one time in our lives so it was fun to have someone to dream of these things about with. He and I dated a few times. He was of the younger generation and man-scaped his genital area. He shaved all the pubic hair completely off and when we would be together it would sting and prick me so much that it gave me a burn similar to a razor burn and I would be sore for days afterwards. On about our third date together he had come down early in the wee hours of the morning and had told his son that he was coming to the beach to watch the sunrise but would be home that afternoon by the time he arrived home from school. Anthony and I were hot together he knew how to perform and did it well, but we were in the heat of passion when suddenly his knee snapped and all I could hear was the roar of his voice in pain from the anguish he was feeling. He froze and told me to be still while he recomposed himself. Slowly he was able to get off of me and lie on his back. He was in tears it appeared to me. But of course he said nothing of how much he was hurting but only how embarrassed he was for having to stop so soon. It hadn't affected me either way for I was so sexually active that one guy not cuming wasn't going make any difference to me one way or the other. I had become, again, a woman with an unquenchable appetite for sex and some would have labeled me a prostitute except I had never accepted a dime from one man ever for sex!

So with the injury we didn't see each other again and I went on about my business continuing to see other men as frequently as I had always been, never denying Franklin or Connery the opportunity to be with me regardless of the number of dates I might have on any given day, they always came first.

There were many men still for me to see, many still emailing me, messaging me on the dating site wanting to meet me.

Grant, the mechanic was one. We never became anything more than friends but even after his persistent approach to befriend me I had finally given in to meet him but he was nothing more than just that to me, a mechanic friend whom I could call if I needed a question answered about my car. He was always there for me for those instances. Grant was a sweetheart and would make the right woman probably the best husband a woman could want, but he wasn't what I wanted in a man. So we stayed friends, never lovers.

Kyle, Paul, David, John, and Tom were just a few more of the many men that would grace my door, some more than others but only a couple would ever make it to the bedroom with me. David and Tom had just enough tenacity to finally get what they were after.

Tom had looked like Popeye to me in a quirky way. He was an x sailor and stood 6'7" tall lean, very attractive and he could cook like no man I knew. He loved to make pies so we always enjoyed making homemade pie crusts together in the kitchen. His arms wrapped around me, kneading the dough together on the cabinet while he nibbled on my neck. Tom was fun in his own way but he was still in love with his last girlfriend and was never able to break those ties with her to commit to a new relationship with me or anyone else so after a while I just let him slip back into her arms where he so desired to be.

David was kinky, he liked to slap and be rough, but he never came to visit me without a beautiful bouquet of flowers in his hands. He was educated and quite formal in many ways. The tall, dark and handsome type, the kind of man I imagined, as the boss at a firm, where the secretary and he would hide away at some local hotel on lunch breaks fucking each other's brains out then returning to the workplace acting like nothing had ever happened between them. David was not my type I wasn't into spanking and tying each other up so we didn't last but a couple of dinners together and oh yes of course the ultimate dessert afterwards!

September was over and Connery had again drifted away. We had not been seeing each other as often for some reason and as October rang in we grew farther apart. I was so into Franklin that I hadn't really minded Connery not being there all the time but had wondered if he was ok. He just never seemed to come clean with me about his life but I supposed by now it didn't matter. I was just going to continue on as I had been and if we broke it off well I would be sad and miss him but I didn't feel like that was it either. The mystery about him had crept back into my thoughts. More than just a little, the presence of his mysteriousness was there a lot now. I had to find out what it was if it killed me. This time I started pursuing information about him from all angles, everything I could do to dig deeper into to finding out who the real Connery was included me digging into his job, his normal routine, his family, the little I knew about them. Still no signs of a woman in his life but surely there was is what I had always felt, but never could be certain.

One day I decided to Google his name again, dig a little deeper into his online history open for the public to see. I found that he had been married to one woman and the address listed still showed Louisiana, there was a second woman on the listing as well, could this be his mother, sister, or was it wife number two possibly? While reading this information about him I read that he had lived just down the street from my place of employment, this puzzled me could this be the man that I had observed often from the large pane windows of the shop? Could this have been him? I had always noticed him on his porch in the morning and the evening after work.

As I dwelt on the possibility of this actually being the same man, I remembered that one of the women I had worked with at that location once had mentioned she knew the couple that lived in that house, the one where I had watched him on occasion outside on his porch.

I decided to figure out a way, indiscreetly as I could to ask my x coworker about this couple, Terry was her name and when she had referenced the subject at hand she had always used the word couple so could this be it, he was with a woman all this time. Now I was determined to find out, get to the bottom of this mysterious man. If he was married I would be devastated for I had fallen in love with him, or with his dick for sure and our encounters. I was addicted to him I couldn't and wouldn't let him go, not yet. I would fight for him maybe even persuade him to leave her and come be with me if possible. What would I do? I was in a state of panic, for if my coworker knew him and as often as she and I had discussed the dating sites and all the men I was seeing how was it I had never mentioned his name to her for that would have blown it all out of the water before we had gotten so involved with each other.

So one day in a casual setting I approached Terry, mentioned that couple and tried to get her to talk about them but she was evasive and too busy to discuss them at the time, so I just dropped the subject. Somehow I was going to find out.

Out of thin air, like someone had just dropped a bomb in the same room with me it came to me. How I might be able to find out more about him, look him up on Facebook!

Facebook, that's how I could know! I would look him up; if he was honest he would have put his birthday, marital status, favorite things and even photographs of himself and his mysterious family on the site for all to view.

I couldn't wait to get home from work that weekend and get on the computer and find him. Even though I wasn't sure of what kind of picture he might have posted as himself I figured it couldn't be too difficult to scroll through Connery Jacksons on Facebook for that was an unusual name and most likely there wouldn't be too many with that exact name.

Upon arriving home I threw down my belongings ran to the computer booted it up and waited to log in to the public forum none as Facebook and see if he was there, married or not married. How would I handle this if he showed himself as married? What if there were pictures of a wife with him how would I really feel? What would I do?

CHAPTER 20

Facebook popped up on my computer screen. I couldn't even read the postings for the day, from my friends. I was consumed with locating his profile and finally once in for all, finding out the truth about him. I wasn't sure if I was really ready to know, but it was past time to open up, to be honest, taking it for what it was worth. If he cared for me at all, it wouldn't matter what I found there on his profile page. I was past the point of caring if there was another woman a wife I didn't care anymore, but I wanted to know so what harm would it cause to finally know the truth after months into the sexual relationship we now had shared.

There was the list of Connery Jacksons, only three listed. This wouldn't take long! I began to tremble with fear. If he was married he might decide to dump me, move on in fear of me tearing his world to pieces, going to his wife! Or even to Terry and sharing the brief slightest bit of information about he and I. Would she go straight to the woman he was with if there was one or just tear me to shreds for having an affair with a taken, possibly married man. I didn't want to know! As I opened up the first Connery Jackson file I knew immediately it wasn't my Connery, for this was an African American man. So I quickly closed and moved on to the next one. Slowly I hit the key to open the next profile, there was no profile picture so I would have to read some of their basic information to see if I could determine if this was him or not.

After reading a bit and viewing a few of the public pictures I realized that this Connery Jackson lived in another State. How had I missed that at the beginning of the profile info?

On to the third and final Connery Jackson, I closed my eyes briefly for I knew, I just knew this was going to be his page. I took a deep breath and hit the button opening the profile picture up, it was him! It was a picture of what he really looked like, not one of those unknown men pictures like so many men had used on the dating sites, as had Connery. It was the real Connery Jackson, the one I had been seeing now for months, meeting daily for sex.

I read his bio, the birthday matched with what he had told me months ago, the location of his home was correct. His education status was all there and correct. As I moved on to the next page of information I read his notations of his favorite TV shows, favorite actors, books, and movies, it all matched with what he had discussed with me on many occasions regarding these specific subjects.

As I got to the final page on his profile I paused, did I really want to know if he was married or not, would I be angry at me, or at him, for living a lie for all these months. I had never sought out to destroy a marriage and the fact that we lived just blocks from each other would make it miserable for me, who knows I might have even met her before, talked with her, seen her in the design store visiting with Terry. Was I really ready for this?

I clicked the tab and there it was as big as the sky "MARRIED", to Abigail Ritchey.

There were a few assorted pictures of her on his page of photos so I viewed each one with pain staking precision and observed everything there was to observe about her. Why had he lied why hadn't he just told me? I was sadden to some degree but as well relieved to finally know the truth. Yes there was a wife, and she had been there all along.

Abigail Ritchey, she hadn't even used his last name as her own. She was beautiful, fair skinned, with beautiful thick shoulder length flowing almost black hair. She had a huge smile, and for all apparent reasons seemed like she was happy. The few pictures of them together were simple posed pictures taken in local locations here on the island. She looked nothing like the kind of woman he always spoke of when we talked about the look of the women he enjoyed being with. He had always said he preferred blondes over them all and he hadn't like the skinny model type, but women with a little meat on them instead. The picture of the wife was just the opposite of everything he had said he liked. Had all this been a lie as well. Had he married a woman that was nothing like his deepest desires, why had they married, there were no children at least he had been honest about that.

What was I going to do? I never set out to destroy someone's life, his especially or now surely not his wife's. I wondered what I would have felt like if William had been in an affair with a woman how would I have reacted. What would I have done, how would I have approached this terrifying new information as the wife of a man cheating for months with another woman. I felt so sorry for Abigail momentarily. I felt deathly sick, angry; a whole barrage of feelings overcame me. I felt sorry for this woman, she had no idea of the turmoil she would soon be enduring in the future with a man like Connery or did she?

His profile noted that they had just been married a couple years, but together for about seven years total. I read and reread his profile information over and over, allowing all the information to sink in, if it ever would.

Now, how would I approach him, how would I let him know I knew the truth? I contemplated options and finally it came to me, of course send him a friend request! A friend request would go to his email address and he would see then that I had found his Facebook page and now knew the truth. How would he react? Would he friend me or ignore me. I would have to face him eventually and we would have the inevitable conversation. But for now this seemed the most indiscreet way to approach him. I knew he was always on the computer and would surely see the email request and know instantaneously that I had found out his mystery, finally.

Sure enough, as I had expected, he never did reply to the friend request. So I would have to confront him in person, rake him over the coals for not sharing that tidbit of important information with me back in June, if not in July at least, when we first starting seeing each other.

Monday was going to be a long day, waiting to chat with him on line, if I did!

What was his motive, why was he on a dating site, why was he a cheater, had she given him reason, to not be the husband he should be? The story would be known soon for he had no reason to lie anymore.

Which one of us would be the first one to open the topic of conversation? It would be interesting to see what happened.

We finally said our good mornings on the chat site, neither of us mentioning the Facebook friend request. I had decided to hold my tongue and let him be the one to bring up the subject of the wife!

My thoughts went back to the first time we had shared our bodies together and the message I had sent him the next day, how foolish I must have seemed to him when he read that message.

"Wow, what a wonderful most delightful surprise, you showing up today! How sweet and special that was for me. I'm not sure what it is about you but you are the most mysterious man I have ever met, but what a beautiful, inspiring, fantastic man as well, I have encountered. I mean that with all my being. I can't pin point what it is exactly but you have me hooked, lock stock and barrel. I must warn you I can fall in love quite easily so don't let that happen with you because I would lose you, you are two perfect and I have already shared way to much with you too fast. I want to experience everything you have to offer a woman from the smallest to the most wonderful thing you can muster. I want you to be mine, and need no one else but me. You have piercing eyes, which can see inside my soul, a cute kissable smile that is irresistible, and the added maturity of that fabulous beard and those locks of soft graying curls for my hands to run through each time we are together. There is nothing I don't like about you, I want you just the way you are! I want to bathe with you, swim nude with you in the ocean, and fly away with you to some exotic location for a day. Hold you tight while sleeping, not waking from this dream, the best dream I have ever had. You have seen me at my worst, and your desires to take me in your arms never faltered no matter how I looked. I cannot wait to know you; all there is to know about you, your life, your work, your family, and your pets. I can't wait to see you tomorrow, the next day and the day after that, every day for the rest of my life if possible. I know being so honest up front may not be the right thing to do but I am hoping that one day we can walk together in the moonlight and make love on the beach, or walk in the rain, kissing as we walk hand and hand as the heavens pour the sweet drops of love upon our bodies. I feel like I am hanging from the highest star and never want to let go I am so into you, please don't let this end I want to be yours forever. Be mine as well?"

Now I wonder how hard he laughed when he read that message. I had opened my heart to him completely, unconditionally. He must have howled.

If my memory served me well his reply was something like this.

"I want to taste you again, feel you in my arms, caress you, taste your undeniable beauty, that so unexpected and completely exciting beauty, you are so gorgeous you have no idea just how gorgeous, you really are."

When he wrote words, or spoke them to me in person, I melted; he knew how to make me turn to putty.

Had he written or spoken to his wife like this? I could only imagine he had. He was good with words, swift, and charming, he knew how to be a gentleman, a player.

He had made my days, my nights, my lunches, he always told me he wanted more of me as much as he could get. He loved my pussy and had no problems asking for more when he felt the desire to have me. Had he done the same with her?

We chatted on line just briefly with no reference to the Facebook request or the subject of a wife. I just never felt right about mentioning it yet and he had completely evaded the subject as well. I made excuses to get off line faster than normal; I needed to think how this was going to work out for me, him, for us, for his wife. It all spelled disaster anyway I read it, it was destined to be a full out disaster.

CHAPTER 21

T uesday rolled around and still no mention of the request, or the wife. He was avoiding the subject like the plaque and I wasn't going to bring it up either, not just yet. I felt he should be the one to make it happen since he was the one who had lied, had deceived me, again. Why was it always, that men felt the need to use you for sex, deceive you with lavish words, gifts, dates, and then tell you it was all a lie?

He had messaged me at some point during the evening on Monday but I hadn't seen it.

"I want you again; you make me get so rock hard in your hands."

"I am going to be gone for a couple of weeks soon and want to be with you as much as possible before I go."

"Please reply when you can. God you are sooo sooo gorgeous!"

Where was he going, when? I was afraid to ask. It didn't matter I was going to lose him anyhow it would all end in time most likely sooner than later.

He was trying way too hard to get my attention, for the first message he wrote me on Tuesday read;

"I'd love to have someone suckle your clitoris as I tongued your rim . . . and together we fingered you, and then finally mounting you and feeling the delicate small fold inside you with my cock. Did you know you had a fold inside? You have such an amazing pussy . . . amazing."

"I know two tongues would work perfectly on you . . . or you laying on your back and each of us suckling a nipple, as together we fingered you . . . and while you reached between our thighs and fondled our cocks. As we knelt on either side of you . . ."

The visual of that almost made me laugh, he was trying way too hard to make me succumbed to his wants, but I wasn't ready to give in. I wanted an explanation I wanted the truth!

"You make me want to just ram my hard dick into that gorgeous mouth of yours."

"Me spurting on your face," "I'd love to fuck your ass while you have a vibrator in your pussy and feel the sensation filtering through to my dick, would you like that?"

I finally gave in, he was making me wet, sloppy, and very horny.

"Yes that all would be so awesome, and fun, but my vibrator is broken so if you want that you will have to go buy me a new one!"

"I am so into you Connery, you just have no idea how much"

"Are you as into me, as I am into you? "I asked him.

"Yes can't you tell?"

"I just needed some confirmation that's all, after all I am still trying to reclaim my confidence from the past and now some new stuff is bothering me."

"Damn faggots!" Your X didn't know what a luxurious gift you are but I do and you can show me how wonderful you are with putting that lovely mouth on my hard dick today for me."

"I can't do anything more than just love you Connery, you are just pure sweetness to me."

"Yeah well, I want my tongue in your sweet ass . . . and my finger in your sweet pussy, and my cock is hungry for both so when can I come see you today?"

"You are hopeless, Connery."

"I have to see you before I go so can I "cum" at lunch today?"

"Alright same time same place, but for now I need to go I will see you at lunch, you know the routine, come in, close and lock the door behind you." "See you in a bit."

So I readied myself for his visit and thought about how it would be now. He had to know I knew he was married but still neither of us had mentioned it not even once.

Lunch time arrived and he did as I requested, let himself in and made his way to the bedroom, but I was in the kitchen, this time so he had to look for me. He kissed me and looked around and made small talk about how clean and neat everything was.

Then he held me tight with his arms and slowly we moved to the bedroom. As we began to undress for the usual lunchtime ritual I noticed his hand, he had worn his wedding ring.

I waited to say anything until we were lying in the bed together and then I just couldn't resist any longer. I had to say it.

"You're married?" "Why haven't you ever told me?" "It wouldn't have mattered at this point but possibly in the beginning it might had. And why now all of a sudden you choose to wear your ring while having sex with me?"

My mind was blown, I couldn't even get into the sex, this was a first.

"Does the wedding ring bother you he asked?"

"Yes of course it does, it's a symbol of your love and devotion to the woman you choose to be your wife, to love and to cherish. Of course it bothers me the fact that we are here together having sex and knowing that your hands that ring have been on me, in me, and as well with her!"

What was I supposed to feel? Like it didn't matter that you are married? It had made me uneasy. The ring made me feel like she was there with us . . . in my bed watching listening, feeling him place his cock inside me, what kind of a man was Connery? Did he have no feelings at all for his wife? I had to know so I ask him.

"I know you are trying to make this easy for me, but I have been completely honest with you from the very beginning, and now finding out that you have lied to me for all these months hurts. I know that sounds like I might be giving up on us but I'm not, not yet, but why, why didn't you tell me?"

He couldn't answer the question at first then he looked me in the eyes and I believe with all his heart he meant the words he spoke.

"Why do women all think love is about fidelity? I'll never get that."

"Because commitment doesn't determine who turns you on, or why and NO ONE can be the most beautiful and alluring person to another forever, it's not possible."

I just laid there listening to him speak. Did every man feel that way?

Had William felt the same way? Was that why he had found Clark more attractive now than me? My heart was hurting suddenly, my William, my William I so missed him . . .

"You have no idea how hard it is to be single and fuck women, and try to remain single! Any woman you fuck wants to get married! Especially if you are good in bed?"

He rambled on and on . . . trying to justify his actions.

I asked him, "Why do you stay with her, do you love her?"

"I'm not going to give you Camille, a laundry list of reasons why I am with Abby, and yes I love her!" "If I was single and available you would feel differently about me and you would want a lot more from me."

"If we were together . . . couldn't we be swingers? Couldn't we date others, even if we were married?"

My first thought was to disagree, but that wasn't what came out of my mouth.

"Maybe, marry me and find out! Leave her and come be mine and see!"

Did I just say that, I couldn't believe that came out of my mouth!

Being with Connery was wonderful, in every way. But I didn't love him; all I wanted was sex from him, his friendship, some of his time. How had I gotten in this situation, with him? He had charmed me right into his own little world and I loved every bit of it. I felt sorry for Abigail; she would be heartbroken if she ever found out. Find out she would, this was a small island and everyone knew everyone else's business or had mutual friends, how had she not already known about Connery and I, or his infidelity.

I never ask him where he was going or for what reason. It just slipped out of my thoughts and the next thing I realized he wasn't on messenger one day. Where was he? Then I remembered and realized we never discussed it again. I had been so absorbed about the wedding ring and the marriage, that him leaving was not part of my thought process for days after that last hookup. Where could he have gone? I would have to wait until I heard back from him to find out all the details. I did know that he would be gone for about two weeks, he had mentioned that.

I used Connery's absence to see more men, spend precious time with Franklin since he had off a few days that first week. I had dates with Patrick, Kyle, Jeff, and TJ during these three weekends that Connery was away. They had all been quite fun. Patrick loved to see his women in ball caps and their flowing hair pulled back into ponytails. My hair was not the good ponytail kind but when with him I had always adorned my head with a cap. Kyle lived in Baytown and it seemed like we always ended up at his little house no matter where we started out at or what our plans were. He was always more comfortable there, besides he drove a fine corvette and it was a sweet ride to be running around town in for all to see. Generally he let the top down so it made it easier for people to notice us. Kyle was a few years older than me but looked great. In the sack he never once could make it happen he'd take Viagra and within minutes he would be hard as stone but with that, came a pounding headache that would put him on his back almost as fast so we never once had intercourse. But what we did have, well it was fulfilling enough!

Jeff was an older man; nice looking had a great body for a man his age. He was tall, lean, and loved oldie Goldie music, we would always go down to the West End of the beach park and listen to the music for hours as we necked and petted in his little car. Sometimes we would go to his sister's house for a roll in the hay. He was always afraid she might know he'd been there so we tried to stay away from there unless the urge just was too strong and we were not able to make it back to my house. Jeff fit me better than any man I had been with, we were like to puzzle parts that fit perfectly together. But there was an important part missing, he wouldn't, and didn't, and refused to, have oral sex, but he sure didn't mind me going down on him. So with that said, I knew it wouldn't last because when I asked him one day in the heat of passion to take me he almost threw up, he turned green said he had never done that, not ever, not even with his wife all those years, well no wonder she ran off with someone else. He'd never done all there was to do with a woman and with some, oral sex was better than penetration. Such a loss!

TJ or better known as Tommy Jay, he was a troll; he looked like a troll doll and acted like one. We had met on the dating site and he had asked me out. This was during the big Bike Rally here on the island and thousands of bikers roamed the streets. He had a troll doll picture on his profile pictures along with a picture of his mom and dad too, strange I thought. But TJ could make me laugh till I just couldn't laugh anymore. I figured the date with him would be great fun. We'd go down to the strand watch the bikes and maybe have a drink or two and who knows what else. But it didn't happen like that at all. When came to pick me up, he immediately said we had to make a trip to the market to purchase limes for he had filled multiple Listerine bottles with Tequila for us to drink so he wouldn't have to buy us drinks while we were out. WARNING, WARNING, should have been what I saw with bright blinking red lights that stated he was a cheap scape. I never saw or spoke to him again after that night. I finally told him to take me to dinner since he had wasted the entire night driving around trying to locate a parking spot where he felt comfortable that no one would break into his precious pickup truck and steal his ridiculous stereo system. If they could have found it underneath the trash piled up in the seats and floor, it would have been a miracle, if it had happened.

Two weeks of interesting fun I guess I could call it while Connery was away. Franklin on the other hand, the days spent with him had been spectacular. I had surprised him by driving to his town. I hadn't ever been to his house so I had to call him to let him know I was there.

At first he was a little peeved I think, but got over it quickly. We went to dinner at a local steak house and then on to his house. It was a nice quite place back off the beaten path, clean almost to clean for a man's home. His TV was in his bedroom so we planted our bodies smack in the middle of the bed and started watching one of his thousands of movies. One thing led to another and before long we were in knee deep, fucking each other's brains out, laughing have a grand time together. Being with Franklin was like being with an old friend, someone you were just comfortable with beyond words. He made it easy for me to like being with him. No mysteries, no pretentiousness, no worries, just good fun and great sex. Franklin liked to play and we could play for hours and hours, before he would ever erupt. Like a spent up volcano he would blow out of control when things got so hot he just couldn't take it anymore.

Franklin had a large pet bird; a Parrot I believe is what it was. It would talk nasty to me and I knew that it had learned those words from Franklin, but I wondered if he had learned them with other women having been at Franklin's house. It didn't matter. I adored Franklin and he knew it. We were not exclusive obviously but he never mentioned ever dating anyone else. Or either he just never felt the need to tell me, if he dated other women or not.

CHAPTER 22

The two weeks had come and gone. I had sent message after message to Connery. He still hadn't replied. I had never called him but I was worried now, it had been long enough I had to know if he was ok. When would I see him again? So I picked up my cell and dialed his number, afraid now that the wife might answer, if so I would just hang up. I'd pressed star sixty-seven before I dialed so that the number showing would read restricted just in case.

It rang, he answered, and I was relieved. I ask him where he'd been, told him I was worried. I was sorry about our last day together and I couldn't wait to be with him again. He began telling me he had been hospitalized for a minor surgery. I was furious why he hadn't told me that was where he'd be. It never came to mind that he was sick. I guess in reality if he'd told me that was where he'd be I might have come to visit him and that might be difficult to explain to Abigail, so it all made sense. We visited briefly and during our short conversation he had warned me if he just hung up it was because Abby had come into the room. Sure enough not but a few minutes had passed and in mid-sentence he disconnected the call. I knew she had walked in.

I wondered what he told her he was doing, who he'd been talking to. Had he made up some crazy answers for her, most likely yes. If she was a jealous type all she would have to do would be, call the cell service and request an itemized bill for the month and every call and both incoming and outgoing would show on the list, along with the numbers. It had been something I had done with William during our "try to make it work" period.

It had been three weeks now since I had last seen Connery. He was still recovering from his surgery. Then one day shortly after our brief phone conversation, there he was. I had seen him on the dating site and I messaged him. I ask when would he be back, out an about? He had replied with his response.

"God you are so gorgeous, I want to feel your body, caress your lips and stick my tongue in your ass so bad. Can I come see you this afternoon?"

I was astonished, was he capable of leaving his home and coming for a visit after surgery? I had never asked nor had he mentioned what kind of surgery he had gone through so it could have any kind. But it must not have been serious enough to keep him confined him from his worldly pleasures of making his women feel happy and fulfilled, I guess!

"Yes, yes, I would love to see you! When can you get here?"

"Give me about an hour and I will be there, we will have to be careful, though. You want be able to climb on top of me!"

What had that meant, climb on top of him? I would know soon enough. I rushed to shower and dress. I was so excited he was coming over it had been way to long! My heart and body had ached for him and for his noteworthy cock to be within striking distance of my pussy.

He showed up early. We kissed like it was our first time. He didn't wait to sit on the sofa and neck he led the way directly to the bedroom. He began undressing me first then removed his shorts and t-shirt. As we climbed into the soft green sheets he pointed out to me the incision on his belly and warned me not to push or put pressure in that spot. It was a significant incision and frightened me enough not to want to touch the area at all.

He laid there with me holding me at first then suddenly he climbed on and placed his solid rock hard dick inside my wet well lubricated pussy, ever so ready for him. He moved slowly but with a rhythm that was igniting my inner fire. He rocked back and forth, then his eyes met mine and I could tell he this was the first time he had made love since we had last seen each other, three weeks ago. I looked at him and asked.

"Have you made love with your wife since your surgery?"

"No, why would you ask that?"

"Because I am worried that I might hurt you, or that you could hurt yourself doing this so soon. What if you ruptured something inside and we had to call 911 or you had to go straight to the hospital, god, what were you thinking? Coming here in this kind of condition?"

"I wanted to fuck you, you have no idea how much I have missed your buxom body, your luscious lips, and that delectable ass. Let's get this done, now!"

We swayed back and forth briefly then he came. It was as if fireworks had gone off inside him he yelped in pain and delight simultaneously. The feeling was mutual. No one was as good as Connery. No one could make me feel so complete and fulfilled as he did. God I wanted him for my own so bad it hurt. I never wanted to not be with Connery, even if it meant destroying is marriage, disrupting his family, ruining his life. I wanted him forever; I wanted to be his Jo Ellen, the love of his life the one he would always care for and have strong desires to be with even until death. I wanted him to love me like George had loved Jo Ellen.

CHAPTER 23

Connery had healed finally and things had gotten back to normal. October had passed quickly with his absence. November was here and so was someone else. Grace O'Brian was her name. Connery had come to me and confessed that he had met someone else. That he had been with her. This had happened after he and I had been together three weeks after his surgery and just before he had gone back to work. This Grace woman had met him on the same dating site as I had months earlier. She had agreed to drive to the island to meet him. They had planned this little rendezvous without ever mentioning this to me. I was angry, hurt mostly that he had wanted to be with someone else. I was well aware that we were not exclusive and was pretty certain he had seen others all along during our months together but he had never mentioned meeting anyone. Only talk of other women in his past. An occasional conversation about a forty year old virgin he had his claws out to get but she would never give in so he had become complacent with her and moved on. Or so he said. I had no hold on him, no wedding ring; all I could think of now was Abigail. She had to know he was a player! How could she not know?

I muddled through most of November best I could. November was the month of my wedding anniversary and Thanksgiving as well. Knowing now that Connery had been with another woman had sent me spiraling into a depressed state of mind. I shouldn't have let it bother me but it did. Why had he felt he needed someone else? He could have me as many times a day as he wanted. Our sex was good together or why else would he keep coming back?

Deep down I was disappointed that I had not been enough for him sexually, especially since he still had his wife Abigail to indulge in as often as he wanted. Why bring someone else into this happy little setting? Oh well nothing I could do would make it go away. I just didn't want to ever have to deal with this woman again. Hopefully one time was all it took for him to realize he had it good, better than most men. She had driven from Louisiana so that wasn't just a little drive it had taken a few hours, so if she wasn't all she was cracked up to be there was surely no way he would care to see her again.

Thanksgiving had passed and houses were beginning to decorate for the Christmas holidays. I just couldn't get in the mood. Holidays were lonely for me now in so many ways. I was alone most of the time, so what was the use of decorating and acting all jolly when there was no one to share it with?

Connery had started coming back over more frequently again. I was relieved and had forgiven him secretly of his whoring ways. We were at my house and he had mentioned that his parents were moving to Texas soon and he shared some of the situations that surrounded the soon to be move. Of course this time he was telling me the truth. For all those other times he had used his mother, family members or whatever, to redirect from having to give it up and be honest about having a wife at home. He had used his family as his excuse to be just the weekday lover.

I had never taken for granite that Connery would always be there for me. To indulge in daily as my needs surfaced for sex. I had decided to get back on the dating site again after the early fall months. Many dates with lots of different men had come and gone. Holidays would be over soon and the New Year beginning and I wanted to be able to maybe, just possibly find a man that I could call my own, someone to fall in love with, someone that would want me as much as I wanted them.

I was browsing the dating site in the middle of the day and I got this message from this man, funny because he was using the same profile name as Connery had used. Strange I thought but when I looked up the listings on the same name there were lots of people using that name . . . so I wondered who this could be. I clicked on the profile and opened up the photograph of the man. Wow what a handsome man. Older, mature looking, balding some, but with longer hair, the beard and mustache I loved on any man. He was sitting at a desk possibly writing something. The photograph showed more of a profile shot vs. a full face photo. He had gotten my attention for sure. I replied, and said hello. Within a few minutes there was a response.

I almost fell out of my desk chair! It was Connery! He was back on the dating site and was using a completely different picture from the one he had used when I met him. I hadn't been logging into the dating site for months and had no idea how long he had been on there and using this picture. What was I to think, had he been there all along. Seeing other women? How could he have held up to this constant rigor of daily sexual adventures with me, his wife at home and now dating site women as well? I was flabbergasted at first, then couldn't do anything but laugh. I had been taken, and taken big time this time. He had used me. But I had used him as well.

We messaged for a few minutes. I grilled him repeatedly about what the hell he was doing and who was this picture of? He didn't have any answers for me as usual. It was like we were starting all over again. Just like it was a new encounter, a new man, a new woman, a new day. In many ways it was all new, this man wasn't Connery, or my Mr. Bond, he resembled Ernest Hemingway in peculiar sort of way, maybe it was the pose, the sitting at the desk. It was so not the Connery I had grown to know to love in my own way. I would play along and see where this Connery would take me in my dating site adventures.

The next day he sent me an email. In this email he had stated he needed someone to care for his elderly parents once they arrived here and wanted me to send my resume to him if I was interested in the job. I had to give this a lot of thought. If I considered this position it would put me right in the heat of his life, family, side by side with Abigail even. Could I do this? I needed employment bad and this could be an answer. I knew him well enough to trust him, or at least I thought I did. I replied, letting him know I would have to think about it. In the mean time I would put together some sort of a resume and a bio-letter that would show my picture and my work history in this particular field, which by the way I did have. He was going to figure out a way to make it appear that he had found my job request on a bill board at work or that a co-worker had known me. He had to convince Abigail that I was perfect for the job. How far was I willing to go? How much more could I do without finally letting on to someone that he and I had been having an affair for almost a year now. I hadn't been able to discuss our affair with anyone other than my closest friends, and I had to make sure in the process that they knew to keep this information to themselves.

December was here, Christmas Eve and I was all alone as I had suspected. I didn't even want to get on the computer for I knew no one would be there. They were all with their families enjoying the special holiday season together.

I logged on the messenger, after a reluctant feeling. Damn there he was, he always knew when to be there for me, must have been ESP.

"Merry Christmas Eve! My dear Bond! How was your follow-up appointment last Thursday? Everything healing ok? I hope so."

"Yeah I'm healing great . . . come suck my dick!"

"You wish, my dear, you come over here to my house and give me a nice Christmas Fuck! You ho, ho, ho.! Wait did you just ask me to come to your house and blow you? I'll be right there! Whatever . . . you'd flip out if I drove up in front of your home in about 5 minutes wouldn't you? I see you're on the dating site as well, finding any hot new woman? I'll be right over you gonna answer the door, or what do I say to Abby when she wants to know what I want when she answers the door?"

"You there?"

"Sure I'm here, so you will come blow me?"

"You didn't read my message did you, preoccupied with the women I assume!" Did you forget to take your meds today? Abby must be at work or outta town for you to go this far, cause you know I'm already in the car on my way!" You shouldn't temp me with such words because I'd be there in a heartbeat babe!"

"I'm going to go now have fun fishing, hope you catch a good one."

"Ha ha, you are too sweet to me, Camille-and so hot!"

"Yeah well I wish everyman felt that way about me."

"They do! What men turn you down?"

"None so far . . . ."

"Other than those damn Gay ones right?" he said

"No they don't even turn me down actually."

"So any luck finding a new hot woman tonight? Where's the wife, working?" I ask him.

"Yeah she's working, and I thought you were going to find me some hot slut to fuck? Until you float back down and I recede from you and crawl up around you and turn you over kissing your brow, damp from exertion as you languidly part your thighs and take me inside you . . ."

"Where did all that come from my dear Bond? That's silly!"

"Blessing me with your body . . . opening yourself to me . . . as I hold myself inside you . . . buried deep within you then I quickly fuck you as I kiss you, and you hold me . . ."

I couldn't help but giggle to myself where was he getting all this crap from?

He continued even more.

"I love thinking about how fucking beautiful you are . . . God I want your hot little ass, your gorgeous rim. I want to feel my cock erupt in your ass . . ."

Again I laughed this time out loud.

"My little ass? Are you sure you know who you are chatting with? Dang your ass is going to all but be gone in another month, with all the weight you've been losing. And you won't want this plump old lady any more when you are lean, buff and tanned."

"You really are so gorgeous! I love fucking you and just looking at you and I love tasting every inch of you."

"Yea, yea, now if I could just sing Opera too, I'd be the whole package!"

"God your gorgeous, you drive me nuts!"

If he only knew how nuts he drove me, he'd probably never gotten involved with me. I had fallen in love with him and trying to deny it wasn't getting me anywhere. He had to know how I really felt. Surely he did. I imagine he made every woman he spent any amount of time with fall in love with him, how could they not?

"Damn I'm coming over there to spank you, right now!"

What was that for I wondered? I didn't even want to ask him so I just left it alone.

"Speaking of Opera, you remind me of that Opera Star, Deborah Voigt. You do look like her you know?"

"Is she the singer that gained all that weight and they threw out of the Operas because she got so heavy? Well I'm not sure if that's a compliment or not?"

"She was beautiful when she was younger, thinner, but you, you have so much more natural beauty than she does . . . and you have such a magnificent build as well."

He sure knew how to make anything sound good. Sometimes I just wasn't sure how to take his comments but I always took them as compliments no matter if they didn't seem to start or end that way when he typed them. I knew he always meant well. I knew he adored me, for he had used that work exactly before. The word adored, only meant that he loved the way I was, not that he loved me. That stung, but he did care about me and no one, not even he would ever make me believe differently.

"You are so Beautiful, Camille inside and out. Don't ever forget that."

"I know Connery you are always trying to make me feel better, make things better for me. I really appreciate everything you say and do for me, honestly but to be perfectly honest with you for once I am scared shitless, about my future. I just don't know whether I will make it or not I know that sounds like I'm giving up, I'm not, I am strong. But this is all so new to me, new territory. I have never been to college, never had to support myself; it's always been given to me. I am not spoiled; it's just the way it was. I was a stay at home wife, and mom. That was the way he wanted it. Now my life seems helpless, no hope. I have so much to be thankful for and don't miss understand me I am not looking for a free ride from any man. I want to work, to maybe even go to college, but I want someone here with me someone by my side, someone to come home to at the end of the day, someone to encourage me along the journey, it's not going to be easy, damn I hate being alone . . . hate it . . . hate it."

"Oh sweetie, I feel so bad for you!"

"Yeah everyone does and that hurts just as bad sometimes . . . cuts me to the core actually. I didn't do anything to deserve this; it's just not fair . . . Connery it's just not fair, damn it."

"Yes I know baby, your X and children should help you."

"Well that will never happen so I won't even go there. I have so much love to give someone. I just need someone to find me . . . or me to find someone, but I don't even know how to do that. I never had to find someone before. The men always came to me. And out of all those men I had to marry the one that would eventually tell me he was GAY! Why me? It's difficult for me to even remember what it was like to be married to him it's like it was another lifetime ago. Honestly I'm not sure I ever even want to remember what it was like deep down. It hurts to bad."

Well we chatted for a while longer then said our goodnights. Christmas was the next morning and I would need to leave early to drive to my mother's house for another holiday as a split family.

New Year's had come and gone and the subject of the job helping out with the parents was the topic of interest again. He had asked if I had made a decision to go work for him or not. I had put together a resume and a bio letter and it was ready for me to forward to his email or fax it to him, however he wanted me to send it I was ready. I had decided to take this opportunity and work for I needed the money, hoping it wouldn't be a really hard job to do. The worst part would be becoming part of the day to day events encompassing all the family events, getting to know his brother, Higgins, aka Higgs and sister Reese. Dealing with the mom and dad wouldn't be difficult it was the rest of the family that frightened me.

CHAPTER 24

We had decided it would be best for me to meet Connery at the hospital room of George, his father. We were to act as if we had never met before, only spoken and that was just in regards of the employment. This shouldn't be difficult to do. I dressed in a nice pair of black dress slacks and a pull over sweater, and light coat. It had gotten chilly out and I wasn't for sure how far I would have to park to make my way to the hospital room on the eighth floor.

I had decided I would be just a bit later than the ten o'clock time we had planned on meeting. I wanted to be the last one to arrive. The other care giver, Celeste Cummings, a friend of Abigail's would be there as well, and most likely Higgs too. I wanted to look professional and knowledgeable of the task I was about to begin.

I arrived and we greeted, right off the bat Higgins had approached me and asked me how long I had known Connery? I looked at him, replied this is the first time I had ever met him. I remember well the comment Higgins said, really, hmmm I would have thought you knew him well by the way you two were so comfortable together. Strange, oh well.

Higgins made me a little uneasy but I was determined I could pull this off for as long as need be.

I would begin work on the seventeenth of January, alternating days and nights as the other caregiver Celeste and myself worked out a schedule between the two of us. Connery had said he didn't care how we did it just that there was always someone there with his mom, Eleanor while George was hospitalized. So Celeste and I worked out an agreement and started working. The first month went ok until Celeste started running late, causing me anxiety. Eleanor wasn't the easiest person to care for; she was a real mental case at times and would all but fight physically if you got in her way or disagreed with her. This might be more difficult than I had imagined. Celeste was working another job and between her and her daughter they shared a car so there was always issues with transportation between the two getting back and forth to the jobs and then there was the kids to pick up from school too. I felt like I was getting the raw end of the deal but I was being paid fairly decent and we could have worked twenty-four hours if we wanted to so if there was a need to make more money all we had to do was work more hours. No one seemed to care.

January slid on by and even though I was working now I still stayed on the dating site as much as I could, and chatted constantly with Connery. He still had the Hemingway look alike photo on the site, but I had no idea why he was even on there for it seemed like there was no time for women anymore, even me. His parents had solved that problem as far as I could tell. I was hurting inside and in need of Connery to be inside me it had been too long. Past time and I had to have him. The work had become almost a burden now for just Celeste an myself we needed help. I had discussed this issue with Connery one night while chatting on line and he had mentioned he might know of someone that might be willing to help out. That was somewhat of a relief. But I had no idea at the time that the person he had in mind would be Grace O'Brian the woman he had met on line back in October, the one he met when he had changed his profile picture and never mentioned to me that he was back on the site in search of new women.

I lost it! Honestly what was he thinking? How could he bring another woman to work in the same home as I? Was he insane? He would surely know that she and I would have a problem working together. We would probably have a time that we would talk and compare our notes on Connery and one of us surely he would favor more than the other. I didn't like this arrangement at all. I had no idea what she might think, but I knew it was going to be hell and nothing I was looking forward to at all. Celeste was difficult enough to deal with. She already figured something was going on I was certain of it. Connery and I were just too chummy when together at his folk's house. I knew she had felt it. And Celeste was close with Abby and probably filled her in on all the unusual things she saw, heard, or felt that were out of the ordinary, when it came to Connery and I, besides Connery had more or less put me in charge and just over looked Celeste. She hadn't accepted that well since Abby had hired her first, she wanted to be in charge.

Now this new woman would be in the mix, and in more ways than one. He called and let me know he would be coming by around lunch time to bring Grace over. I was to show her around and fill her in on the day to day procedures. God this was not anything I wanted to be a part of. Noon time was approaching, I freshened up my makeup and hair I wanted to be looking my best when Connery showed up with her and I wanted to make sure I was prettier than her. I had no idea what she looked like. I had never had enough gall to ask him.

He knocked, they walked in, I stood frozen, and my mouth must have dropped wide open, as my eyes met his. Grace was like an Amazon woman, six foot tall at least, large boned natural blonde, no makeup, simple and homely looking woman. She had worn a ragged white t-shirt and a pair of jeans that looked like they were the only pair she owned and wore them every day. A huge sigh of relief came over me. I had worried about nothing! He introduced us to each other, we said our hellos and he turned to leave, but before he left I made sure she saw me give him a kiss, a kiss on his lips!

No more than a few minutes passed by and I started the conversation, asking how she had met him and how long they had known each other. Her story was unbelievable, for she proceeded to tell me the exact story that Connery and I had established incase Abby had asked at any time how he had found me. I couldn't believe what I was hearing. He had obviously instructed her to use the same story. She had no idea that I had used the same one. I let her know quickly that I knew where they had met and that he and I had met at the same place and that we had been seeing each other for almost a year now. I immediately told her that he was married as well . . . just in case she had no idea, she wasn't going to get too far if I could help it. She had begun to share with me their first encounter.

They had met on the same dating site and the one difference was Connery and her had used Skype so they had video chatted and she had known right from the get go that he didn't look anything like the latest photo he was using on the dating site now. We talked about the one visit she had made here to the island back in the fall to be with him. She didn't mind sharing the details with me at all. She spoke of how they had met locally and had driven to the East End and had sex in her car. Once done she had driven back to Louisiana that same day. Was this for real? I would have to question Connery about this. It was difficult for me to believe that anyone in their right mind would drive that far just to have sex with a stranger. Besides that, she had told me that while they had been chatting she had noticed his wedding ring and she knew he was married and didn't care. I didn't understand how anyone could come that far, have sex, drive back home and all this time know that the man she was meeting was married what did she have up her sleeve. Something wasn't right about this. There had to be more, more than what she was sharing at the moment and a hell of a lot more than he had ever shared with me, a whole lot more.

This day just happen to be the first Friday of Mardi Gras and Connery had purchased tickets for all of us to go if we wanted to. He needed us to help push George around in his wheel chair and someone to watch over Eleanor. The only reason he was going was Abigail was in the parade and he had to go watch her do her thing. He had called me, confirmed that I would be going and had given me the details when and where to meet them at, that would be him, Grace, George and Eleanor. I had agreed and arrived in the parking garage early so I could make a grand appearance in the condo for I had dug out my lace black top and the barely nothing black lace bra to wear. When I opened the door Connery's eyes lit up and he couldn't take his eyes off me. I was stunning looking and I knew it! Grace made a nasty little comment something of the nature that she wasn't aware that we were going to dress up for the evening. I just smiled for I knew if it came down to looks, and probably "job performance" I would win out in both. There was nothing attractive about her in my opinion.

We walked down to the garage together and then he turned to me out of realization that my car was the only car that would carry them all. So I handed him the keys and I climbed in the back seat behind him so that he was able to view me in the rear view mirror while we drove downtown. Grace didn't like me at all, I could feel it. And that was fine with me. I knew before long something negative would happen between us and I knew that I would go straight to Connery with whatever it was. He had to know that this was not a good situation, to put two of his "women" working together with his family. Again all I could imagine what had gone through his mind when he had asked her to come work here with us.

We made it to the downtown area. Connery parked the car after letting us all out. Once he caught up with us we immediately started walking through the vendors booths and checking out the merchandise being sold. Connery had noticed a booth selling boa's so he purchased a hot pink one for me while I was attending to his father in the wheel chair. Connery approached me with the gift and placed it around my neck while whispering, he thought I might be cold and this would keep my neck warm. This was the first thing he had every bought me with the exception of the taco and soda he had paid for months before. I was so pleased and proudly pranced around flaunting the new pink boa for Grace to see. She wasn't as excited about it as I was, of course. The pink boa would be something I would cherish forever. Little though it might have seemed to others, it had meaning to me, a place and time that could always remember a good time had.

We made our way through the crowds finally sitting waiting for the parades to march through the streets. Once they were all done we headed back towards the car and Connery picked us up and drove us back to the Condo. The evening had been exciting, interesting and even a bit overwhelming in many ways. I had felt like Grace and I would be forever competing for Connery now. It would be a daily ordeal between her and me. I was worried that if it got too far out of hand that Connery would just dump us both. I was going to make sure that if any one got dumped it would be her, not me. I would do or say anything within my being to keep Connery for myself, even though I might have to share him with others I was not going to let this woman destroy all that he and I had worked so hard to obtain.

I departed from the garage without even going back up to the condo. There was no reason and besides I was tired it had been a mentally exhausting day, meeting Grace O'Brian was more than I thought it would be and then the parade and dealing with the folks as well. Tomorrow would be a new day. I could start fresh and new with the emotional ordeal of dealing with the third wheel, Grace. I went on to work as usual aware that she wouldn't be there until time for me to leave from my shift. Little did I know I would be wrong? Connery had asked her to come over while I was there so she could observe the day in and day out routine. Get familiar with things. I was frustrated of this information. I wanted to be rid of her and bad. So she arrived shortly after I did, but it was nothing like she had expected things would be. I had already done the morning chores, meds and anything else I could think of. I wanted time to sit down and talk with her, get her side of the story from beginning to end. We did a few little reviews of the daily tasks and then Grace and I went back to the back room sat down and began talking. We discussed the dating site, her profile name, how long we'd both been on the site and a few odds and ins. Then I asked her when she had met Connery, what picture was he using at the time and how many times they had been together sexually. She didn't hesitate to share the answers to all the questions I had laid out in front of her. It was like she knew it would happen and was fully prepared with answers.

Grace had met Connery back in October just after he had his surgery. She had driven to the island just as he had said to meet up with him to have sex. The stories of both so far matched.

She had also shared, just as Connery had instructed me with the resume and job for her to do the same. Then she begins to tell me how she had been left for dead basically in storage shed where her husband had run off and left her. She had managed to get away and was living with a close friend now and needed work and Connery had offered her the third shift position and she had jumped at the opportunity. She told me of her life and how she had been used, and abused by all her x's three to be exact, the third not yet divorced and no date in site. It amazed me that men and women could just fuck around while married. I must have been brought up with some strict moral beliefs because I would have never been able to do these things if I had been married; it was hard enough now sometimes even being single sleeping around. Times had changed from when I was a teenager and sleeping with complete strangers was normal to most.

Grace begin telling me how she had video chatted with Connery and how she had noticed his wedding ring on one occasion and had questioned him about it then. He had been honest with her and yes, told her he was married, and happily at that, but he just needed sex with others and often. It hadn't seemed to bother her one bit. She mentioned her children and grandchildren and her idiot sister, as she had called her, Satan, in female form. She hated her sister it was obvious.

Finally she said something that caught my attention. Something I had to even ask her to repeat again just to make certain I had understood her correctly. She had sat there on the bed in the home of Connery's parents and boldly looked me straight in the face and said that from this point on . . . She would be included in the family will. She was going to make sure that the husband and wife, the one plus one would now not equal two but three, meaning that she was going to bust up this marriage, she would take her place as his and the wife would be good riddance. I couldn't believe my ears. I was shocked had he known this was what kind of person she was, probably not. It wouldn't be long before he would because I was going to make sure he knew this. She was after his money, his life, and wanted him. She would do anything and everything to have her way. I wasn't going to let that happen. I had been there first, and even though I didn't want Connery or his money, nor to destroy his marriage I did want him for sex and for a friend and I would fright for what I had gone through to get to where I was. If I had known in the beginning he was married I would have never gotten myself in this situation but it had happened.

Connery was made aware of Graces preexisting pretenses. He wasn't happy about this little insight regarding the newest employee. He should have checked her out better. With me he could have gone to anyone on the island and questioned my integrity, my intensions. But with her he had nowhere to check, it was her word or nothing.

Things got better in time and we settled our differences and she found out that Connery and I cared for each other in ways she had no idea. I wasn't going anywhere anytime soon.

CHAPTER 25

February and January had been stressful months. The new responsibly of caring for Connery's parents, meeting Abigail, Celeste, and then there was Grace, much less the folks and Higgs too. Had I gotten into something I didn't have any control over? Or was I in complete control and no one realized it yet but me.

Connery, had he been a complete fool by placing me in the position of caring for his parents, meeting his wife, brother, and becoming a part of the day to day routine in the Jackson family lives? I had wondered if he thought at some point, I could turn on him, tell the world of our affair and now could include the so called one time sexual encounter with Grace O'Brian as well. He'd better watch his p's and q's as the old adage went for if he decided to not see me anymore I had a hold of some pretty important information that I was certain could and destroy his little perfect world, as he knew it. I had been used to seeing Connery so many times a day that I was having withdrawals. He was like an illegal drug and I was so addicted to him I would do anything to have him, to taste him, to have his body.

Connery hadn't realized that I was capable of telling all, if push came to shove. For the moment we were still alright, but I still wanted him sexually, now even more than ever. I also wanted him to have nothing to do with Grace for she had become a real bitch. She did nothing when it came to actually working at the folk's house and it seemed like all the real work still fell on Celeste and me. So he was paying Grace to sit and play on her computer games or talk on the phone or hunt for willing men on line throughout the day to meet up with her. It wasn't right. When I had gone to him, telling him of her don't give a damn, attitude he snubbed me in a strange way or it at appeared to me as if he had. This angered me, the first time I think he had ever angered me, and he'd better watch it was all I could think.

I was in the position to burst his bubble, destroy his world. But I wouldn't do that to Connery even if he pushed me completely away, or never saw me again for sex, I still couldn't hurt him. I had fallen in love with him and nothing or no one would take that from me. I would always hold a place in my heart for him. Once he had told me if he ever had to move away, leave the island, he would forget about me in time and would move on to the next woman. That had cut me deep, but he if he ever left the island he would then have no reason to want me to need me, all we had in common was put into simple words with one of our messaging conversations.

"You are a gorgeous woman, and you have no idea. You are so hot, I adore how gorgeous you are, but if I ever leave the island you would be just like all the others, history. I would forget about you and move on to the next one. There would always be someone in my life to supply the unconditional sex that I so craved. Abby had lost my attention like I had told you once before, that no one can have an alluring attraction to the same person for a life time, it's not meant to be that way."

This hurt me, but I knew I would do the same with him, at least the move on part, but I could never forget him, my Mr. Bond, my GCLST. With no regrets he would forever be a part of my life and I wouldn't have it any other way.

He knew just what to say to a woman, how to treat her. He was the perfect gentleman in more ways than one. He was an exquisite specimen of a man. And I had told him so.

"Hello gorgeous! What ya wearing? Knowing you not much I'm pretty certain!"

"Hi there handsome, you're right, pretty much naked at the moment. What ya doing?"

"Just a working boy today. God I want you so bad right now. I don't have a lot of time today but I want my dick in your mouth."

"I want to see you too, Connery, really bad! Can you make it by this afternoon for a quickie maybe? Is Abby working tonight? I won't be home until a little after six p.m. as usual got to close the store up this evening."

"I'll see. Yes the wife's working. I love seeing you, Camille. You might need a good spanking *grin*." He had typed.

"I love being with you so much Connery . . . I wish I . . . never mind . . ."

"Uh-oh, were you waxing romantic there for a second? *grin*.

"Yeah, don't laugh at me, what a shame that I have let you in that far. I should have never allowed that to happen. Guess I am feeling a little melancholy today for some reason. I am generally much more cautious with my emotions than what I have been with you for some reason, dang it's just not right."

I thought of Rolando briefly, how I had fallen so deeply under his spell last summer. William had been the worst when it came to putting a spell on me; his had lasted a life time and now look where I was."

"You should know how I feel about you Connery after all these months, you should know by now."

"Well my experience has been that women rarely are so open with their sexuality as you have been. I just love how gorgeous you are in my arms, how you give yourself to me so freely so unconditionally. Not wanting anything more than just my sex and a bit of my time."

He had been right in so many ways. I didn't want to marry him, he wasn't marrying material. I felt so sorry for his wives, the first and second one, and especially Abigail, since she too had met him on a dating site and had won his love and his heart. He had left wife number two to go be with Abby. How had she done that, she must have been good at persuading him to leave his life and come running into her arms as her own.

"I hate that that once a woman shares her sexuality with a man they normally want you all to themselves . . . I hate that you have to choose just one! I love Abby to death but I will never just want her, there will always have to be others to share my sexuality with even if it's behind her back, sorry to say."

"Why had you married her then, you loved her enough to marry her, since you did I assume, obviously she was the right choice since you are still with her and can still see other women without suspicious inquiries from her. It seems like it works to me, I don't care as long as she shares a little of you with me . . . it's all good, right?"

"Ha-ha . . . well, never to her . . . but . . ."

He drifted off from his thoughts and the subject changed. Suddenly he brought up a subject that had never been discussed before between the two of us. He had suggested I should write a book, a book I thought, about what?

"You should write a book, Camille. Telling of all your adventures with men, tell the world how your faggot x had destroyed your life and you kids, wouldn't come forward and help the woman that have given them life. Family should stick together in times like this. You have been given a raw deal, and you of all people don't deserve to be the bad one, to be treated like this. You are so beautiful, so wonderful any man would want you for his own. You just need to find the right one, but it's not me. I am not the one for you I never will be. I am not the right man for any woman not even Abby. Sorry to say!"

"A book, OMG you have lost it Connery, I have never written anything before with the exceptions of a few sexy, erotic poems for Franklin at Christmas time. He always loved them though and always asked where I'd get the ideas to write those words on paper from? Maybe you are right Connery maybe I should write a book, a book about you and me! How we met the adventures we have gone through. The deception of the phony pictures you placed on the dating sites as a married man and on the prowl looking for sex! Yeah that sounds like a perfect idea."

"Poems for Franklin, really let's see one. Let me read one if you have a copy still. Maybe you are supposed to be a writer, you never know. Some people have to be pushed into situations that they never suspected they would ever go to become what they are meant to be. So let's read this erotic poem."

"Really, you really want to see it, to read it? It's quite unusual and a little long but it tells of our adventures my feelings for him. If you really want to read it I can email it to you."

So with that said I forwarded to Connery the Erotic Poem I had written for Franklin. It was a strange feeling for Connery to read how I felt about Franklin and to read of our silly sexual acts that were so different from he and I.

"Okay here you go . . . let me know what you think about it."

I love you Franklin
But I know you don't love me
If I died tomorrow at least I would know
The words in my heart have been set free!

I treasure the moments we have spent together
Drinks, dinner, laughter, and well . . . whatever
I adore the way you are so kind and tender
I crack up when our words turn to banter.

Franklin, the man's man
All who know you, know you can
Be a macho man, in time of despair
Or as I know you, a pussy cat, that always seems to care

You can make me pee . . .
Make me laugh, with orgasmic convulsions
Make me cum, with your tongue,
With tons of emotion
Go on and on and never be done!
Contrary to others
You always get the job done.

I can spend the night with you
And never miss a minute sleep
Share a dinner with you
And never say a peep

Dress in rags or dress to the hilt
No matter where we might go
Don't give me a dare,
For only you know that I will flash in a heartbeat
My breast I will bare!

I love to look deep in your eyes
And See a man who makes me think twice
Feel your warmth flow so freely from deep inside
And never doubt that you are my friend come rain or come
    shine!
With a desire always to be by my side.

I love to hear you laugh
To watch you play with yourself
To suckle my tits, and eat my grits!
Caress my thumb deep within your ass,
Oh what a hoot, has been . . . our past!

To bend over in rest
Do you attest?
That the rear end
Is always the best?

Your dick is so sweet
And gives me such delight
Ooo . . . even, when sometimes it, I might bite
Never in spite, but always
Such sheer delight.

Or place a small rod within you so deep
Always wondering if you will stop me
Before it goes beep beep?

You know where to touch me
You know how to feel
The inside of my bladder
So much better,
Than any doctor, ever will!

I enjoy riding your face
Even, when I fart in disgrace
With my ass in your site's
You never blink twice, or wrinkle your face!
When golden showers fall from within
You only open wider to swallow till its end

For what are friends for
If we can't be who we really are
Just one big ole bunch of fun
When in my arms,
Is what you are!

I hope this never ends
The wonder of it all
I know with you it all depends
If you get that damned ole work call

I would cry to see you go
I would miss you so
So please don't go
If you stay, I will let you suck my toe!

Temptations whether enticing or not
You're a man I can never forget
Take me with you
If you leave
For with you, I would never cheat or deceive

With all these silly words
I say, just to you, be of much concern
If you have to go, a hard lesson I will learn
And know deep in my heart,
Most likely, you
Will never return.

But I wanted to make you laugh
Before this Christmas is gone
With memories of our past
To know that you are happy
Once and for last!

Even though sadness will in gulf me if you go
I leave you with a thought to ponder, and please
Don't forget me or my desires
Cause someday you might have to eat my pussy again,
Does that somewhat inspire?

For my love for you, is real
So sorry you feel, it's no big deal
To quote you once again, my Franklin
Damn it . . . LOL,
What a ride it's been!

All the love I have to give
Is at your fingertips, just call my name
Just say the word, and I will be there
To bring you much cheer

Merry Christmas and a Happy New Year, My wonderful Dear
    Friend!
May our journey never ever end!
For I have no regrets
From the day it began.

So this wraps it up for this year
No tell'n what might happen
In the New Year
But I know in my heart
It can only get better for you have been here
And are with me forever!

All my love, forever and ever
For it's been my pleasure!
From beginning to End!

So there I had forwarded a private moment between Franklin and me to Connery. Would he think it was insane, stupid? Probably so, for poems just didn't seem like it would be one of the things Connery got off to, but I wouldn't know unless I let him read it and got feedback from him. I waited to hear his comments.

"Wow, I'm impressed! That's really good. Not sure what it all means but I can tell it was coming from your heart. It's a little long but poems have no limit so, not bad, not bad at all. Maybe you should really consider writing; seriously, it could be your calling."

With that I had decided what harm would it do and I began the book and the title would of course have to be "Hello Gorgeous" since all this time he had always addressed me with those words, it only made sense to make that the title. So I set out on a journey, yet another journey I had never been down and I owed it all to Connery Jackson, the man that had been the inspiration from the beginning when I first laid eyes on him that Spring day and then when we finally met for the first time in June. He had been the same man that I had viewed from my workplace windows all those months ago. He had lived across the street and I had always thought how handsome he was. Little would I know that we would end up together enter twining our lives in so many ways. He would continue to be on the dating site for months and months to come. It never bothered me after Grace came into the picture, when other women would vie for his attention, for I realized that he was a free spirit and no woman not even me would ever tame his animal soul, his hunger to migrate from woman to woman.

I had fallen in love with Mr. Bond. I met him as Ernest Hemingway and would go on to even know him in a third profile as Indiana Jones. I had summarized Connery in the end as a man of many faces. I had forwarded to him a few years later that I had categorized him as an actor. My personal actor always there no matter what face he wore or what profile name he used he was always and forever my Mr. Bond. I had shared my thoughts with him regarding those first three profile pictures and my summation of who he was acting out to be with each new photo he had used. This is what I had sent him.

Ah . . . Let's see if I can do this . . . here goes . . . in my own words . . . . a magnificent man, vibrant and full of life!

In profile one you were my James Bond, suave, sophisticated, and sexual beyond belief. A true "Gentle" gentleman in every since of the way, a real live "Gold Finger" forever in pursuit of his "Pussy Galore"

In profile two you were my Earnest Hemingway, intellectual, somewhat eccentric, a private man with an eye for the realistic needs and desires of a woman and the know-how, to fulfill these desires in a wide range of complex emotions in your own succinct style. You are at the pinnacle of the game when it comes to knowing how to lure a woman into your arms and suck them right into your novel of life.

In profile three you were my Indiana Jones, handsome, full of adventure, exciting, always turning over every stone looking for the perfect gem of a woman, a woman that could make you more of man than what you were, if that is possible. With each encounter you treat your woman as if it were your "Last Crusade" and your last living, breathing, feast.

In real life you are an adorable man, sweet, extremely giving, a "Gorgeous" man, gracious in more ways than I could list!

All in all you are as near perfect specimen of a man I could have ever dreamed of encountering in my lifetime. From large Santa to a perfect "10", clean shaven or full beard, long soft curls or short cut hair, and finally completely bald. You have encompassed it all. Who would have ever known it all started with these two little words "Hello Gorgeous."

It has been my pleasure to have met you, to have caressed your warm body, too have kissed your sweet mouth, to have been one with you often and even now to continue to be friends with you so many years after. Life has been forever changed because of our encounter; the bar of expectations has been raised.

For anyone other woman that might have had, or might have, the opportunity to meet you, they should do so with unbridled, wild abandoned freedom. As a free spirit ready for a flight into the heavens as if they were Lois Lane with their arms wrapped around Superman climbing to heights unreached. It could be the ride of your life if you allow it to be.

That was how I had felt about him after the end of the first few years, moving on into our next year's together now.

I had been on the dating site one afternoon still single in many ways and having slowed down quite a bit now with dating and all the sex, with the exception of Franklin, who was still around after all those years and memories of all the magnificent times I had spent with Connery, after all the years of being with him, when on this day, there on Facebook, I received a message from a dating site. I wondered who it could be from. I opened it up and there he was, "Gentle Fun" requesting to be my friend.

Connery! He was back at it again, on the hunt, on the prowl for women. Would he ever be satisfied with just one, his wife number four now, and probably well on his way to wife number five soon enough, most likely not? I replied with a yes to accept his friendship. With that we started again, another dating site game, another profile. New encounters of sex and meeting behind closed doors. Soon afterwards he messaged me.

"Come pick me up!"

"What, come pick you up? What on earth for?" I asked him.

"Just come get me lets go for a ride, I'm on the bicycle so we need to go in your car."

"Ok give me about thirty minutes and I'll be there, same place? Will you be outside waiting on me, or should I call you when I get there?"

"Call me!"

So I left to go get him, down at the port gates, where guest could enter and leave without complications. Connery had deceived me as well in many other ways, he wasn't from Louisiana he had never even been there. He had moved to the island from the West Coast, employed with large Oil Company as an analyst. It had taken me years to find this information out. It never really mattered to me, for he could have been a bum living on the beach and I would have still fallen for his Sean Connery looks and his sweet smile.

We drove to the beach, parked where no one was at, and no one could see us. We necked for a while; it was so good to taste his sweet warm mouth again. I gave him a blow job; he spurted all over me and his pants. It was so good to be with him again, it had been months and months. I had missed him so!

We started again, a new adventure of sex, indiscretion, and so many things that just weren't right. But I had one advantage this time, I knew who he was, I knew the real Connery, finally. After all we had been through together, the affair all those years ago, jobs, and the book, the death of George, and now another divorce, and my commitment to Franklin, for the time being.

He had me left alone, lonely all over again to fend for myself, all those years ago. He was so comforting to be with again, a secure familiar feeling. We drove back to his work place once we were done, and when I drove up to let him out at the port gate, he leaned over, gave me a soft kiss goodbye, said to me,

"Can I see you again? Tomorrow possibly when I get off work? The wife is working late nursing shift and I can come to your place if you have no plans? I want to taste you again, to feel your soft body against mine. I want to hold your hands tight within mine when you orgasm for me while I am deep inside you, feeling your soft gentle fold and kissing your beautiful breasts. God you are sooo gorgeous, I want you for lunch, dinner, and for desert. God . . . you are so uniquely beautiful so so sooo gorgeous, you just have no idea how delectable you are."

Our affair would begin again, I felt it in my bones I would forever be a part of his life, I would forever, be his "Jo Ellen." He was just like his father had once been; he had met a woman that wanted nothing more from him than just the encounters for sex no strings attached just a fulfilling afternoon of lunch break sex. For now and until the end of time, I would gladly consent to being his secret woman if that would make him happy. For it would be all I needed to complete my world, unless Franklin every found out and left me. These were the two men I had desired so desperately for in the beginning, for such different reasons. Fate would have it that my wish had been granted. How I handled it would depend on me.

Rendezvous' from here on out would be exciting, a new adventure. I would have to hide them from the man I had finally won as my own, Franklin. But Connery, oh my Connery he was never going to be without me. Deception, sex, men, nothing would ever change, except now it was me deceiving myself for I knew Connery would never be mine and I would be risking the love of Franklin, deceiving him, by succumbing to the sexual desires and wishes of Connery once again.

"Rendezvous again, same time, same place, Thursday? I'll be waiting for, you . . ."

Was the message he sent me after getting back to his office.

"God you are still so gorgeous . . . . even after all these years!"

Upcoming Book!

"Rendezous"

Same time. Same place?

I'll be wating for you!

Sherry J. Cook

My opinion was if any married man had balls enough to get on a dating site meeting women just for sex then he wasn't much of a husband to have around. Besides, I wasn't the only woman that had been with Connery, so had Grace! Maybe she was more worried about herself than what might happen with Connery and his wife. Oh well, I didn't really care anymore. She was history and I didn't care if I ever saw or spoke to her again. Reality would have it that she would eventually leave the island, and the country even, with that skank of a man she had been sharing three other women with for months on end. Living the lie, that one day maybe he would be hers and hers alone . . . .

CPSIA information can be obtained at www.ICGtesting.com
Printed in the USA
LVOW050225130712

289900LV00002B/45/P

9 781477 227756